MIXED TO DEATH

A BETTY SNICKERDOODLE MYSTERY (#4)

PEPPER FROST

WORKING STRATEGY

MIXED TO DEATH

Hardcover Large Print ISBN: 978-1-970044-08-9

Paperback Large Print ISBN: 978-1-970044-17-1

For my mom 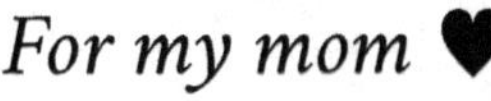

CHAPTER 1

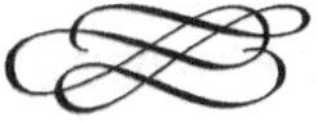

The afternoon sun warmed Bea Sickles' old bones as she puttered about the grounds of her wine-country inn in a threadbare nightie and little else. Betty Snickerdoodle's Christmas Inn & Ranch—the property she'd purchased months earlier with the millions she'd made writing Betty Snickerdoodle books—was practically vacant, and the ranch's ample acreage meant she was far out of sight of any neighbors. Bea could enjoy the balmy morning weather as she pleased, with no need to worry about disapproving busybodies tsk-tsking about the unrestrained body parts running amok beneath her translucent sleepwear.

Not that she would ever have worried anyway.

Well, perhaps she would have worried just a smidge. But only because Angela Garcia, her brilliant young friend and the president of their company, Betty Snickerdoodle, Inc., had been gently nudging her toward more socially acceptable behavior—at least where apparel was concerned.

Angela had happened upon an irrefutably persuasive argument: If anyone complained, Bea could get arrested for indecent exposure. Even that might not have deterred Bea, though, if not for a recent stay in a holding cell at the police station. Bea's jail time was short, but the memory of it gave her pause.

Not enough pause to make her put on a robe, mind you. Not when the sun was so glorious and the spring air in Napa Valley so invigorating! But enough pause that Bea stayed close to the inn, a good thirty yards away from the road. This was hardly a sacrifice, since that's where the prettiest flowers were, blooming spectacularly in beds outside the windows of the guest rooms of her charming holiday-themed inn.

Bea's favorite place to enjoy the fresh air and the greenery and the flowers was right underneath the picture window of her very own suite. She knew from looking out that window that it had the best view of the ranch and the neighboring vineyards. Bea loved the vantage point so much that Angela asked a carpenter to attach a flip-down bench under the window. The narrow wooden slab blended seamlessly into the wall when not in use, but Bea could unlatch it whenever she wanted to enjoy the outdoors in her preferred spot. The bench had become Bea's favorite place to plan devious and inventive ways to end the lives of characters in her recently launched mystery series—a new pastime that brought her endless delight.

As Bea enjoyed the feel of the grass between her gnarled toes and the sweet scent of the lilacs that had bloomed out of nowhere in mere days, a vehicle sped into the driveway. It was a small, boxy van, elaborately decorated in a soft pink and white design that seemed at odds with the vehicle's rugged shape. The driver steered the vehicle assuredly past Bea to the far end of the parking lot and braked to an abrupt stop with a squeak and a creak.

"Zoom, zoom," Bea chuckled to herself. "Looks like somebody's got important business to attend to."

As the van cruised by, Bea noticed a nearly life-sized image of a bride and groom on its side. A logo in ornate lavender script proclaimed

"Marry Well Wedding & Event Planning." A website address and a phone number with a Sacramento area code were displayed underneath.

Bea grinned as she watched a broad-shouldered woman about six feet tall exit the vehicle. She had short, brownish hair and a large Roman nose. Her ill-fitting pantsuit looked businesslike and uncomfortable. Her age was hard to peg, but Bea thought she could be anywhere from late thirties to late forties. The woman headed straight toward the entrance with complete focus on her destination, striding past Bea as if she weren't even there.

"Howdy!" Bea said, waving her hand melodramatically. A breeze caught the hem of her flimsy nightie and exposed her spindly legs—and very nearly her undies. "Oopsie! That was a close one," Bea cackled hysterically. "Can I help you?"

The woman clucked her tongue and kept walking, her left eye beaming disapproval at Bea like a laser.

Bea snorted. "Ha! I get ya. Have a nice day, madame." Bea held the fabric of her nightie on either side of her body and made an ostentatious display of curtsying.

The woman stopped and turned around slowly. A mix of disgust and impatience flashed across her face as she looked down at Bea. The woman's lips curled inward and her brows furrowed. When she opened her mouth as if to say something, nothing came out.

"Cat got your tongue?" Bea said, chortling again and pointing behind the woman. "Or look—maybe it was a puppy."

The woman turned to look where Bea was pointing. A well-dressed, pretty woman with an elegant bob was pushing a stroller holding four adorable, yipping puppies down the trail from the winery next door. The puppies' mother, a miniature dachshund with a long red coat and an exquisite face, trotted alongside the carriage on a leash.

"Maybe you can help me," the tall visitor said breathlessly as she rushed to the woman behind the stroller. "Are you affiliated with this inn?"

"Not—not officially. I'm Connie Hollander. I'm the owner of the property next door, Heavenly West. But I'm—"

"Thank goodness I ran into you," the tall woman interrupted. "My name's Rhonda. Rhonda Butts. I'm a wedding planner—high-end weddings. I came to meet with the manager, but I'm tempted to turn around and head back to Sac." She leaned in and added in a quiet, conspiratorial tone, "I've heard a lot about San Francisco's vagrancy problem, but I had no idea it had infected the wine country." As she said it, she tilted her head in Bea's direction. She leaned toward Connie again, then looked from side to side. "She hasn't set up a tent, has she?"

Connie looked at Bea, her eyes wide. "I think… I think there's a misunderstanding—"

Bea laughed diabolically as she listened in. "Did I hear you say 'Butts'?"

Rhonda's eyes opened wide as she sucked in a lungful of air and leaned backward. The expression on her face grew even more severe, which only made Bea laugh louder.

Rhonda turned her back toward Bea. "I'd like to get away from here A-S-A-P, Connie, if you know what I mean. Do you think I can find the manager inside? Should I just ask at the front desk?"

Connie peered around Rhonda and glanced at Bea nervously, then looked back at Rhonda. "I was looking for Angela myself—it's Angela Garcia you're looking for, right? Why don't we go inside and find her together?"

With apparent relief, Rhonda headed swiftly towards the entrance of the inn. Connie looked sheepishly at Bea and shrugged, then turned the stroller around and followed Rhonda toward the front door.

"Hey wedding planner lady, wait a minute," Bea yelled after them. "I'm sorry if I alarmed you. You look like a successful professional woman."

Rhonda eyed Bea cautiously and paused, her expression relaxing a bit. "I'm impressed that you noticed," Rhonda said.

"How could I miss it?" Bea grinned. Her tiny body slightly hunched, she moved toward Rhonda with her arm extended. "Anyone can appreciate your impressive image—dare I call it 'commanding'?" Bea was smirking and staring at the gap in Rhonda's jacket, where a large, silver filigree button strained against her formidable bustline. "Plus, look at that fancy vehicle you've got for your business. You must be doing something right."

Rhonda couldn't suppress a smile. "Well, thank you. Perhaps we got off on the wrong foot." She reached her hand out in the direction of Bea's.

"Indeed," Bea said, opening her palm as her hand reached Rhonda's. "So, rich lady. Can you spare any change?"

Rhonda clenched her fist and snatched her hand back, turning on her heel to head toward the inn's front door.

"I'll take that as a no, cheapo!" Bea shouted. "You know, you're not very nice. I was just asking for a small donation. Besides, what kind of person doesn't even notice the world's cutest puppies? Even I think they're cute, and I'm an old crank."

Bea was cackling uproariously now. No one enjoyed Bea's sarcasm more than she did. The piercing sound of her laughter floated on the gentle spring breeze.

Connie looked back at Bea and smiled, stifling a chuckle, then followed Rhonda into the inn.

"Please don't tell her anything, Connie," Bea hissed. "Don't spoil my fun!"

CHAPTER 2

"*N*ice to meet you, Ms. Butts," Angela said, smiling and extending her hand upward to shake Rhonda's much larger one. Angela was dressed crisply as usual, in pressed black jeans, sleek flats, and a white linen blouse. "I haven't thought about hosting weddings at the inn, but I'm excited to learn more about it—"

"Like I told you on the phone, my elite brides always ask about wine country venues. I'm always looking for new options," Rhonda said, scanning the features of the inn's large ballroom as she spoke.

"I'm delighted you called! I don't know much about wedding planning, but it seems like such an uplifting profession. You're helping couples with the most important event of their lives," Angela gushed. "Do you love your work?"

"Huh," Rhonda said gruffly, pulling a tape measure from her pocket. "I'm sure you can fit at least three hundred guests in here."

Angela cocked her head and furrowed her brow. "I'm sorry, I thought I mentioned from the start that our capacity is two hundred and fifty. Our permit is grandfathered to match the prior owner's—"

"Yes, with plated dinner, two-fifty sounds right, but we could easily fit three hundred, maybe three twenty-five for passed appetizers only. We're in this to make money, right?" Rhonda was pointing at imaginary spots on the ballroom floor and counting under her breath, a hungry look on her face. "I think we could fit more than enough high-top cocktail tables for three hundred and twenty-five. How many will the deck hold?"

"Probably fifty or maybe seventy-five at a time, but those would be included in our permitted maximum, which like I said is—"

"That deck will be a draw for photos. Beautiful backdrop of the foothills and that old winery—"

"Heavenly West, you mean?" Angela said. The dreamy expression returned to her face as she envisioned a joyful wedding party posed in front of the pretty view from the deck.

"Whatever that place is," Rhonda replied with a quick wave. "And the other direction, too, with that red barn and the vineyard across the road. Brides'll eat that up with a spoon. You could make suites available for the wedding party, in case anyone needs to touch up their hair and makeup, right?"

"Of course," Angela said. "We've got the casitas, too, for more privacy. You know—I've heard that the bride will want to be sure she's not seen by the groom before the ceremony."

"Huh," Rhonda grunted again. "Good idea—I bet we could do ceremonies here, too. Nice. The bigger the packages, the bigger the percentages," Rhonda said, grinning and rubbing her thumb and fingers together. Then the imposing, lavishly decorated tree in the corner of the ballroom caught her eye and she scowled. Her eyes darted back and forth from it to the massive wreath above the fireplace, the smaller trees on the ballroom's large stage, and the many other carefully designed Christmas decorations adorning the room.

"Shame you haven't done anything with the Christmas trees—you do know it's been months since Christmas, don't you?" Rhonda said, her face a mixture of disgust and pity. "You'll make sure they're removed before our mixer, I presume?"

"Rhonda, this is Betty Snickerdoodle's Christmas Inn & Ranch. The inn is inspired by the Treacle Town series of books, and it exists for Betty's fans. Christmas trees are an integral part of our branding—"

"Just as I suspected, a marketing issue," Rhonda said. "The good news is getting some weddings on your calendar could turn this place around. Don't you worry, Angela."

"I wasn't—"

"And the better news is you'll have access to my valuable marketing advice—my friends call it 'million-dollar marketing advice,' but you'll be pleased to know I don't even charge for a lot of it. If we add your facility to our inventory, that is. Then it's a win-win for me to help you get your facility marketing up to snuff."

"Facility?" Angela said, taken aback. "We aim for such a warm feeling here. I don't know if I think of our inn as a 'facility'—"

"You'll learn a whole new language if you join the wedding industry—only if you're interested in success, of course. As in bookings," Rhonda announced. One side of her mouth was raised in a victorious smile. "This location is perfect. We could charge a bucket of money. All those rich brides will want first crack at a new wedding venue. Almost forgot to ask, does all the load-in happen through the front entrance? That might be a problem. Any other entrances for vendors to move their gear in?"

"We've got a side door, and caterers can enter through the back of the kitchen. Can I ask what type of vendors—"

"There will be rented tables, linens, DJ and sound equipment, lighting—that sort of thing. There's also the catering, the bar, and the cake. Sometimes photo booths, chocolate fountains. High-end weddings have a lot of moving parts. And plenty of flowers, of course. High-end brides love their peonies."

The wistful look returned to Angela's face. "Peonies are those big, fluffy flowers, right?"

Rhonda didn't answer. Instead, she pulled out her phone. "We'd better start planning our industry mixer—the sooner we introduce the vendor community to your facility, the better. We've got an unexpected opening coming up in a couple of Thursdays—can't imagine you've got anything booked, what with those Christmas trees gathering dust. Can we lock it in?"

"The date sounds fine, I think. And you said we

don't have to do anything to prepare for the mixer?"

"That's the great thing about hosting a network of wedding professionals. We take over and you know your facility is in good hands. Oh, except for those unsightly Christmas decorations. It goes without saying you'll have to take care of those."

"About that, Rhonda, just to be clear—"

"Good. Why not start now? You know, my crazy old auntie was a hoarder, and she kept a lot of old stuff around longer than she should have. Couldn't bring herself to get rid of any of it until she found out she was dying. At least she did clear the C-R-A-P out in time to enjoy her last few months," Rhonda chuckled. "Come to think of it, that might not have been the most fun you could have when you're dying, but at least none of us had to deal with her junk after she was gone."

"Rhonda, the trees—the Christmas decorations —they're not *junk*," Angela said patiently. "Just to be clear, they're part of our holiday theme décor—"

"I'll email you the mixer proposal later today. Get it back to me fast so I can round up the troops. Must scoot, I've got another meeting back in Sacramento. Oh, and one more thing, Angela—

a rather big thing. Do you know you have a suspicious-looking vagrant hanging around the grounds?"

"A vagrant? Really? Of course I'll look into that, Rhonda. That's never happened before—"

"I trust you'll get security for the mixer. It's included in our agreement," Rhonda said as she flounced out the door with a wave, moving so fast she didn't even notice Connie peering around the door, listening in.

"Come on in, Connie," Angela said. "You heard all that, I guess."

"I started to leave after I escorted her here, but I just couldn't resist. She's something, isn't she? Am I right that it sounds like you're going ahead with the mixer?"

"I don't have to do any of the work," Angela said, "and it sounds like weddings could be a great business opportunity. Can't hurt to at least learn about it, right?" She sounded like she was trying to convince herself as much as Connie. "I do think my mother needs to explain how she could refer Rhonda to me without any warning whatsoever, though," she added with a laugh.

. . .

"OK, SPILL IT," ANGELA SAID. SHE WAS SITTING AT her desk, smiling at the pretty face of her mother, Maria, on the laptop screen in front of her. Connie sat behind Angela on the end of the bed. "What's the connection between you and Rhonda Butts?"

"I only just met her this morning. It was at that flower shop I love," Maria said. "The one owned by that lovely British lady, Fiona Wheaton."

"The English Rose in Gold Country? The shop in Fair Oaks?"

"That's the one. Not too far from your old stomping grounds at Sac State."

Connie smiled and waved at the camera on the top of Angela's computer. "Hi, Maria!"

"Connie, are the pups with you?" Maria said. "Can I see them? Have they got names yet?"

"They're right next door, in my suite. I can go get them if you like—"

"Mom, Connie can give us a puppy update later," Angela interrupted. "First, you need to finish telling me how you sent that… that… shall we say *unusual* woman my way."

"Right. Sorry. I was shopping for an arrangement—a housewarming gift for a client who just closed on a house. I love those generous, English-style arrangements they do in that shop. While I was explaining what I wanted to Fiona, you'll never believe who walked in."

"Rhonda?"

"No—George Peterson!"

"That's a blast from the past," Angela said, mouth agape. "Wow. Gorgeous George."

"Hmm," said Connie. "Sounds like an old boyfriend. Should I keep this conversation from Aseem?"

Aseem, the tech whiz who was Angela's right hand in managing Betty Snickerdoodle, Inc., was also her devoted boyfriend. They'd been together since mid-winter, after many months of denying their ardent attraction and compatibility. Aseem had done most of the resisting. He'd been worried about how they'd balance their intense feelings with working so closely together on building a company.

Maria and Angela giggled simultaneously.

"He has nothing to worry about. George is short for Georgina," Angela said. "She was my roommate in college. We worked at the same company for a while after, too, but we lost touch when I moved to San Francisco. She picked up George as a nickname freshman year and it stuck. The guys all started calling her 'Gorgeous George.' Naturally, she loved that," Angela laughed. "So what's George up to, mom? Is she as beautiful as ever? Still a completely free spirit?"

"She works as a wedding planner now. Still stunning, but honestly, I thought she looked a little tired. Or maybe stressed. She asked about you, of course. I was just starting to tell her all about Betty Snickerdoodle and the inn, when who should walk in but—"

"*Now* let me guess," Angela laughed. "Rhonda?"

"Yep. Rhonda rushed over and interrupted us. She latched onto 'inn' and 'wine country' and asked if you do weddings. She said that there aren't nearly enough wedding locations in the wine country to meet the demand."

"That's what she said when she called me," Angela said. "She hadn't even heard of Betty Snickerdoodle, but she was absolutely certain the inn would be the perfect reception site for her 'high-end brides.' Whatever that means. She seemed to think it means we all get rich quick."

"I'm afraid she got the bit in her teeth and took off running. She said she was going to call you right away about setting up some kind of wedding industry mixer. I didn't know that meant she'd call you the second she left the shop—much less drive up to see you today! I'm sorry, honey, but I couldn't really refuse to give her the inn's number.

Especially not with George there—I mean, Georgina. I don't think she goes by George anymore, by the way. She seemed uncomfortable when I called her that."

"The inn's not exactly a secret, Mamá. Don't worry about it. Rhonda's a bit strange, but… I'm glad you gave her the number. But what about George? *Georgina,* I mean—boy, that's going to be a hard habit to break. She's a wedding planner, too?"

"Georgina and Rhonda work together. I thought Georgina started to say she was Rhonda's partner, but Rhonda talked over her and described her as a sort of apprentice. I felt bad for Georgina. She looked disappointed. Once she got your number, Rhonda herded Georgina out the door. When they were gone, Fiona told me—very diplomatically—that she finds Rhonda a little overbearing. And what was the other word she used? Daft. 'A bit daft,' to be exact."

"Understatement—that's a British thing, right? Maybe 'daft' is their version of 'bless her heart,'" said Connie, exaggerating her own Southern twang.

Angela snorted. "I'd go with 'oaf.' Rhonda kept telling me she couldn't understand why there were so many Christmas decorations at the inn in

May. She also promised to help me 'learn how to market' the property."

"I thought you held your composure very well. I couldn't have done it," Connie laughed. "But you didn't even see the best part, Angela. When Rhonda arrived to meet Angela, Bea was outside on the grounds—in her nightie."

"Dios mío," Maria said. "I don't even want to guess—"

"Wait, so Bea was the vagrant Rhonda complained about?" Angela blurted, bursting into giggles.

"Oh, Angela," Connie roared, "Bea laid it on thick out in the driveway. She made a good show of panhandling."

"Looks like I'll have to explain to Rhonda who Bea is—"

"Hope it goes better than when you tried to explain about the Christmas decorations."

"I'm sorry there wasn't time for me to warn you about Rhonda, sweetheart," Maria said. "So did you tell her thanks but no thanks?"

"I know it might sound crazy, but… I think we should have a wedding mixer here. It can't hurt to learn about the wedding business, can it? What do we have to lose? And Rhonda says—well, you already know that Rhonda says it's very lucrative, and besides, she promises to handle everything. She says she gets a select group of vendors—florist, DJ, catering, etc.—to donate their services for a party for the wedding community. They combine their networking with a chance to come check out each other's latest offerings—and our place, of course."

Through the laptop display, Maria's face crumpled slightly. "I'm sure… I'm sure you can handle Rhonda, honey. I just hope she won't give you too much trouble."

"That's what the mixer's for," Angela said. "To learn if we can work together, right?"

"But Angela," Connie said with mock solemnity, "what are you going to do about the Christmas trees?"

"Nothing!" Angela snorted. "I'm hoping the other vendors will notice the sign saying 'Betty Snickerdoodle's Christmas Inn & Ranch.' And if brides don't like Christmas, why should they get married here?"

"Cheers to you, my friend," Connie said. She stood up from the bed and opened the door connecting her suite to Angela's. The puppies' mother immediately trotted in. "I thought I heard you at the door, Bijou," Connie said, reaching down to stroke the pretty dog's head.

Her four tiny dachshund puppies bounced in after her.

Connie picked up two of the pups and showed them off to the camera. "Puppy time!" She lifted the one in her left hand, a female with long, red hair, closer to the lens. "This is Garnet."

"She looks just like her mother," Maria said. "Garnet's a perfect name."

Connie switched and showed off the girl in her other hand, a short-haired red pup who wriggled energetically and let out a playful yap. "She's called Paprika."

"Cute!" Maria said, hands on her cheeks.

Angela picked up the other two—male pups with short, black-and-tan coats. "Here's Jonathan." Jonathan was the largest of the four and so placid, he seemed sleepy in Angela's hand.

"He's an old soul," Angela smiled. She switched and moved the other, smaller pup closer to the camera. "This little guy, not so much. We named him Damien—Dames for short." Dames was wriggling and yapping like his sister. "Dames and Paprika are going to be troublemakers when they get older."

"Have you decided which one you're going to keep?"

"Luckily, I don't have to for a while," Angela

said. "Connie and the dogs are staying here while they build Connie's cottage next door."

"It's a dream solution for me," Connie said. "I've got another trip back to Kentucky soon, and I don't have to worry about my furry brood at all while I'm gone, thanks to Angela."

"It's my pleasure, truly," Angela said. "Is your trip all business, or will you have some fun, too?"

"Mostly business," Connie said. "But I love it so much, it counts as fun."

Connie was heading up a new business for her family's company, the bourbon-maker Heavenly Mash. A few months before, she purchased the winery next door to build Heavenly West, and now she was building a home on the property, too. It had been a fantastic development for both Connie and Angela. Though Connie was a bit older, they shared many interests—including making their own mark in business.

"Ladies, it's been fun, but I've got a house to show," Maria said, waving from the computer screen. "But before I do, mija, I've got a question for you. Fiona called me today. She said she noticed the barn in a picture on your website. She wondered if you'd discussed it with Rhonda. She thought it might be perfect for more intimate weddings and farm-to-table dining."

"Rhonda was only interested in big, fancy weddings," Angela said. "Events with a couple hundred people or more. We only toured the ballroom."

"OK if I tell Fiona to call you? She said she had an idea involving the barn that you might be interested in."

"Of course. If you have it, can you text me George's number, too? Arggh, I mean *Georgina*," Angela said with a laugh. Then she blew a kiss at the screen. "Bye, Mom. Love you."

CHAPTER 3

Angela scanned her unanswered emails. At the top of the list was a third one from Fiona Wheaton. Angela smiled at the polite way Fiona tried to coax her to reply. "Perhaps you missed my earlier emails?" read Fiona's subject line.

Angela understood why Fiona was anxious. The mixer was coming up soon, and Angela still hadn't confirmed that Fiona's barn proposal was a "go." Angela had been stalling, holding out hope her little plan would work. She picked up her cell and texted Georgina Peterson again to suggest a video chat. This time, her old friend surprised her and wrote right back.

```
ok. sure. sorry. been busy w
weddings. can u send link?
```

Without wasting a moment, Angela fired up the chat and sent Georgina a link. Her laptop chimed and Georgina's face filled the screen. Her big blue eyes and blonde hair were as striking as Angela remembered, and her pristine bone structure seemed even more stunning.

My mother was right, Angela thought. *She does look a bit tired. Still gorgeous, though.*

"If it isn't my old pal George Sandpiper. Or maybe George Sandwich!"

Georgina's uncomfortable chuckle was exaggerated by the slight delay in the video. "That's me," she said. "The old me, I mean. I prefer Georgina these days."

"I'm sorry. I know. My mom told me. I just can't help remembering our glory days."

"Glory days?" Georgina scoffed. "I'd say you're in your glory right now. From what I hear, you're in charge of the inn and who knows what else. Don't you know people are buzzing about you in the alumni network? Everything seems to have worked out like a dream for you, Angela."

"It was a lot of hard work," Angela said, a bit

injured. "But I was lucky to be hired by Bea, I'll admit. Her books are a marketer's dream."

"Those Betty Doodle books are big hits."

Angela smiled. "Betty *Snicker*doodle. I guess you haven't read them."

"You know I was never much of a reader. I barely read enough to get by in college. I couldn't have gotten through it if you hadn't helped me with some of those classes. Reading for fun is definitely not my thing."

"I remember," Angela said. "I studied enough for both of us. It was a fair deal, though. If it weren't for you, I wouldn't have had any fun in college."

Angela began to relax, feeling the rhythm of her old friendship with Georgina returning—at least she hoped so. "Anyway, the Betty Snickerdoodle books had already sold hundreds of thousands of copies when I started working for Bea, and we bumped it up to millions. That's where all the money to buy the inn came from."

"Sounds like easy money," Georgina chuckled. "I'm sure it's not, though. No offense."

"Bea always says, 'It's a tough way to make an easy living.' She told me that's what all the poker pros say. Did you know she was a professional poker player years ago, before Betty took off? I think the saying fits the bestselling author business, too. It's a nice life. But speaking only for myself, it's also been a lot of work."

"What's the idea you wanted to tell me? Sorry I haven't had time to call you."

"No worries. But—surprise, surprise—the idea is related to weddings. You know Rhonda's planning a mixer here at the inn, right?"

"Of course. I'll be her backup—I mean, her partner. I've been helping with all the planning."

"How would you feel about an extra responsibility? Fiona Wheaton—the English florist—needs someone to lend her a hand. She's going to be doing an additional, special display—"

"No offense again, Angela, but that can't be true. Rhonda would have told me. She controls all the displays at the mixers."

"This will be separate, located elsewhere on the property. Surely Rhonda doesn't expect to dictate everything," Angela said, struggling to find a light tone. "Fiona wanted to do something apart from the mixer, to promote the new organic flower farm she's starting."

"I heard a rumor about that. She bought a farm near Placerville, right?" Georgina said. "Fiona's on the fringe of our industry. Hears the beat of her own drum, Rhonda says. Perfectly nice woman,

I'm sure. We just haven't done much business with her."

"This might be a chance to get to know her better—if you want, I mean," Angela said. "She asked about our little barn. Have you seen it on the website?"

"No—I'm sorry—like I said, so busy—"

"Please don't worry, George—Georgina. Here's the thing. Fiona wants to set up a display of her flowers and decorations in the barn, as an example of how a wedding reception in the barn would look. Fiona told me barn weddings are a thing—"

"They are."

"I thought it sounded strange when she said a wedding in a barn can be fancy. But she had ideas not just for her organic flowers, but farm-to-table catering—"

"Sounds good. Seems like she has it figured out. Where do I come in?"

"She told me that she'd bring in a wedding coordinator to help her with her display. And then I remembered my mom said you were apprenticing with Rhonda, and I thought if you were thinking about striking out on your own, this could be an opportunity for you. I'd benefit, too, because I could trust you—"

"And you could feel good about helping poor little me," Georgina said. "Reaching down from your pedestal, offering your hand to pull me from the bottom. You can call it 'giving back,' I suppose. Must be nice."

Angela felt her face flush. "I didn't mean it like that. I know you've made a big success with Rhonda. I just thought—"

"I'm sure you mean well, but you're misunderstanding. I'm not just an apprentice—I started that way, but I've been with Rhonda for a while now. I am sure I'll be made a partner any day." Georgina glanced downward and paused. "It can't hurt to hedge my bets, though, I suppose."

Angela smiled. "So you'll do it?"

"I'll need to clear it with Rhonda. Will you let me handle that? It's not like I can't make my own decisions. I just don't want any alarm bells to go off. I need to make clear that I'll give her whatever help she needs with the mixer," Georgina said. "She says there's a lot riding on this opportunity at your inn."

"Yes, of course you should handle telling Rhonda. I'm excited you want to do it! It's been so long since we worked together at that first job. Remember?"

"How could I forget? You were the star pupil, of course. Kicked my butt there, too."

"It wasn't a competition, *Gorgeous George*," Angela said. "Sorry. I can't help it. You were still going by George last time we talked. Fun times, weren't they?"

"I guess they were. But look at all you've accomplished. It's time for me to get serious, too. Georgina's a grown-up name. Time for me to use it."

"Georgina it is," Angela said. "Don't worry. I'll get the hang of it. Shall I tell Fiona to give you a call?"

"I've got her number. Once I work things out with Rhonda, I'll call Fiona."

"Sounds like a plan!"

CHAPTER 4

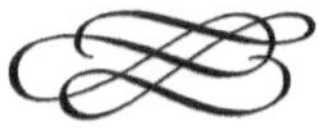

"It's exciting, isn't it?" Angela said. A dreamy look brightened her face as she set up a book-signing table for Bea on the lawn near the entrance to the inn. Bijou nosed around quietly in the grass, leash dragging behind her. In honor of the networking event that would soon begin in the ballroom, Angela had swapped her jeans for pretty linen slacks and a sleeveless blouse. "The wedding mixer, I mean. Learning about weddings. Not that your book signing isn't exciting, too."

"Oh, boy." Bea let loose a cacophonous laugh. "You're getting wedding fever."

"Of course not! Aseem and I have only been together a few months. But I've hardly been to any weddings. Can you blame me for being a little fascinated? They're one of life's guaranteed joys, right? It's an industry that pulls together so many fun things: fashion, flowers, food. And family and friends. What's not to love? Plus, I'm looking forward to seeing my friend George again. Georgina, I mean. I used to know her as George."

"Sounds like a juicy story," Bea said, leaning in. "Tell me more."

"It's not that exciting. Just a college thing. We had this women's studies class, and we were reading about authors who took male pen names—"

"I know. *Middlemarch*, right?"

"I'm impressed. You've studied feminist history."

"Not hardly. I learned it from Jeopardy! They have clues about those female George authors at least once a year."

"Should have known. But you're thinking of George Eliot. It was George Sand who gave Georgina her nickname."

"I see," Bea said, yawning and stretching theatrically. "Right again, Angie—this story's a lot less exciting than I expected."

"We had fun coming up with pen names Georgina could use. George Sandwich was my favorite, because of the late-night snacks we'd get at the food trucks."

"Angie, how could you have concealed this wild-child history of yours? You're such a goody-two-shoes now. What a U-turn!"

Angela rolled her eyes. "George and I had our fun. Truth be told, though, George was more your speed. You two would have been great friends in college, right up until you both got expelled. I helped her avoid that, and she taught me to loosen up a little. It's been a few years since I've seen her. She's a wedding planner now. She's actually Rhonda's assistant—or apprentice, I guess."

"Lucky girl."

"I know, that's why I set her up to help Fiona with her barn-wedding idea. Who knows? Maybe Georgina can break free of Rhonda and start her own business, working with Fiona. The barn-wedding idea sounds charming."

"What about Rhonda? You sure you're not kicking the hornet's nest?"

"We're smarter than Rhonda, right? And I think Georgina is smarter than Rhonda, too."

"Everyone's smarter than Rhonda, girlie. But hornets aren't that smart, either. Doesn't mean they can't hurt you."

Angela shrugged and opened a big box of fresh

copies of Betty Snickerdoodle's wine country mystery, *A Killer Uncorked*. She piled the books neatly on the table, along with a few pens for autographing. Then she set a bag and a rectangular metal box on the ground beside it.

"Check out the new sign," Angela said, smiling. She pulled a small handle from the top of the metal box, unfurling a colorful vinyl banner. The banner stood nearly five feet tall and featured a huge, bold headline ("A *Killer* New Series from Betty Snickerdoodle") and a photo of the book, with a charming image of the inn and its neighboring vineyards in the background. A partial caricature of Bea's face was set on the edge, so that it looked as if Bea was peering around a corner and winking at the viewer.

"I guess I'm really out of the closet now," Bea frowned.

Angela laughed. "Surely you're getting used to it by now."

Not even a year ago, Bea's anonymous, reclusive existence had been disrupted when a bumbling crook stole an unpublished Betty Snickerdoodle manuscript. The chain of events that followed forced Bea out of hiding—but led to new directions for her author business, too. Given a choice, Bea surely would have continued her hermit lifestyle. But the inn, the interactions with fans, the mystery writing—it had all turned out to be a lot of fun. Her new notoriety even presented opportunities to dominate a few choice poker games. In a candid moment, Bea would easily admit that she was much happier in this new chapter of her life. However, this was not such a moment.

"Whatever. I guess the sign's OK. You have your style of promotion, Angie, and I have mine." She unzipped the jacket of her track suit to reveal a baggy gray t-shirt with a custom message: *I Kill People for Fun and Profit!* Underneath the headline were images of a vial of poison, a smoking pistol, and a dagger dripping with blood.

"Definitely on-brand, like you marketeers say," Bea snickered.

"It's a little aggressive, but OK…. Too bad they didn't have your size."

Bea zipped her jacket back up. "It's an extra-extra small. A little roomy, but you know I don't like my clothes too constricting. The point is the message. Besides, you got your wish. I'm not plan-ning any other gags today. I'm not even pulling a homeless prank on Rhonda. Mainly because I couldn't think of a good one."

"I'll take what I can get," Angela said. "You all

set for now? I need to check on the pups. They're alone in Connie's suite. Who knows what they've been up to."

"Will you leave the poochie mama to keep me company?"

"Sure. One last thing," Angela said, pulling a wireless card-swiping device from the bag on the ground. "In case anyone wants to buy a book. Remember how to use it?"

"All good," Bea said, plopping down into the chair behind the table. "I'm not anticipating a run on books. No one's even looking my way."

"Give it time, Bea. The vendors are all busy setting up," Angela said, turning and walking back to the inn.

"By the way, Angie," Bea called after her, "I'm surprised you didn't notice I'm wearing my bra! Just like I promised."

"I'll alert the media," Angela shouted, without looking back.

Bea looked down at Bijou and snickered. "Angie's sarcasm game's really improving, don't you think, Bijou? I'll take credit for that." She leaned back in the chair and waited less than a minute for something to happen. "OK, I'm bored already. Oh hurrah, I spoke too soon. Here comes fun!"

A familiar vehicle barreled around the bend

toward the driveway. Bea quickly wriggled out of her jacket, smoothing the front of her t-shirt. "This will be a primo opportunity to promote my message."

Rhonda's "Marry Well" van sailed into the driveway and screeched to a halt near the grass where the table stood. Rhonda hustled out of the cab and slammed the door. She looked over the hood impatiently and yelled at Bea, "Where the H-E-double-hockey-sticks am I supposed to park my van?"

Rhonda spread her arms in the direction of the parking area to underscore the obvious: every spot was taken. Vendors had crowded near the inn, using hand trucks to move boxes and displays from their vehicles into the ballroom. Some vehicles were even double-parked for unloading.

"Oh, no!" Rhonda said, suddenly realizing it was Bea she was talking to. "No! No! No! I can't believe it. It's you again!"

"Almost like I never left. Can I interest you in a book?"

Rhonda walked toward the table, her head shaking slowly in disbelief.

"This is an unpleasant surprise." She picked up the credit card swiper and sneered. "You're begging for credit card payments?"

"Haven't you heard? We've become a cashless society. Even us panhandlers have to pivot."

Rhonda shook her head and made a noise like a grunt. "I told Angela we must have adequate security for our mixer."

"And she told you I own this place. One of you two doesn't listen." Bea cupped her chin with her hand and after feigning a thoughtful pause, she let loose another gleeful cackle. "Spoiler alert, Rhonda: It's you!"

Before Rhonda could respond, a nondescript economy car pulled in behind her van. It had a security strobe light flashing on its roof, the cord dangling from it into the driver's side window. A sturdy-looking woman in a security guard's uniform quickly exited the vehicle and headed toward the table.

"Is everything OK, miss? Is this woman bothering you?"

"Finally, some evidence of security," Rhonda said. "Better late than never. This... this... woman is interrupting our event." She pointed at Bea's face and glared. Bea rewarded her with a smirk. "She seems proud of being a degenerate. Look at what she's wearing!"

"I mean *Miss Sickles,* are *you* all right? I'm sorry I'm late."

"It's OK, Pat," Bea chuckled. "But maybe you could try explaining to Rhonda Dimbulb here that I own this joint. She thinks I'm a trespasser."

Pat Rogers was a private detective friend of Bea's. One of Pat's favorite private-eye accessories was her all-purpose security uniform, which helped her slip unimpeded into almost any under-cover situation. It was working like a charm again. The twenty-dollar mall-cop light on the top of her car completed the look.

"Ms. Dimbulb, I can assure you Miss Sickles signs my checks. And that's her pen name, Betty Snickerdoodle, on the sign right over there," Pat said.

"My name is not Ms. Dimbulb!" Rhonda said, her face reddening.

"Pardon me," Pat said. "No offense. Is it Mrs. Dimbulb? Miss?"

"You better calm down there, Rhonda," Bea said. "You look like you might pop one of those fancy buttons of yours." Rhonda's suit was sim-ilar to the one she wore the last time she'd been at the inn, but in a different color. It had been customized with the same filigree buttons, and they were once more straining across her bustline.

Rhonda's face progressed from red to purple.

"Security guard—Pat, is it?—perhaps you can tell me—"

A short, middle-aged woman with a soft, endearing face interrupted Rhonda with a shout as she hustled toward the table from the inn entrance, waving and smiling. "Oh my goodness! Is it really you?"

"Of course it's me, Sandy. Duh!" Rhonda said, throwing up her hands.

"Not you, Rhonda," the woman said with a friendly laugh. "I mean, is that really Betty Snickerdoodle? I just love your books!"

"In the flesh," Bea said.

"I want to buy a copy of your new mystery. I've heard it's a page-turner. Can I come back later with my credit card? I also brought some of your Christmas books from my collection. Would you mind signing them?"

"It would be my pleasure," Bea said. "But please call me Bea—that's my real name. And I love your t-shirt. Reminds me of mine."

Bea stood up from behind the table to show off the murderous message on her shirt.

"I love it," Sandy laughed, holding her fist up for a bump with Bea's. "Great minds think alike?"

Sandy's shirt said "I Shoot People and Sometimes Cut Off Their Heads," with an old-fashioned SLR camera under the text. The name of her company, Sandy Givens Photography, was printed on the back. "People take themselves so seriously in this business. I say we should have a little fun when we're networking. Of course, I'm serious as a heart attack when at an actual wedding."

"What a treat to get autographed copies from a bestselling author," Sandy added. "And to see your beautiful inn and ranch, Bea. Thank you for the group room rate! I wouldn't normally splurge on an overnight stay. And I don't think I've ever been to an industry function here in Napa—thanks for making it happen, Rhonda. I must say, I wouldn't have pegged you for a reader. Are you secretly a Betty Snickerdoodle fan?"

Rhonda snorted and turned to Pat. "I need a place to park my van so I can get inside that ballroom and oversee this event. Who knows what else Angela forgot? Got any ideas?"

"There's overflow parking at Heavenly West next door. It's about a ten-minute walk on the trail back to the inn. If you prefer to ride, one of the limo companies is providing a shuttle. I'm also happy to drive there with you now and give you a lift back—"

"Let's go," Rhonda said, striding toward her

small van. Pat led the way up the hill to Heavenly West in her compact car, the amber security light still spinning.

"Apology accepted," Bea shouted after Rhonda, prompting a laugh from Sandy. "Rhonda's something else. How'd she get to be in charge of your group?"

"Probably because no one else took the reins. She's not so bad. The key's not to get enmeshed with her little clique of favorites. I hear that once you're in, you can't get out," Sandy said, raising an eyebrow conspiratorially. "I was lucky enough to have built up my business years ago, before Rhonda started trying to control everything—I mean, before Rhonda took on such a prominent role. Most of my business is referrals from happy brides. Newer vendors around here seem to rely more on other vendors for referrals. I've always thought that creates conflicts of interest. But I'm old-school."

"Interesting business. Everyone depending on vendor word-of-mouth gives the bullies a foothold," Bea said.

"You can buy advertising, too. Most of us do. But a good reputation is key. Honestly, I hear people whining about Rhonda, but I just tune it out. If you get involved in the drama, or tangle with her, nothing good comes of it. Like the owner of that limo company your security gal mentioned—Destination Dream. Rhonda had a squabble with him a while back, and let's just say Dennis didn't win."

"No wonder she jumped at the chance to have Pat drive her back from next door," said Bea. "Not many people would choose Pat's old econo-box over a limo ride. What's Rhonda got against Destination Dream? Why are they here if Rhonda doesn't want to do business with them?"

"The second question's easier," Sandy said. "There aren't that many limo companies in our little network up in Sacramento, and it's not cheap to send a driver all the way to Napa for the night."

"Surely we have limo companies around here. Let me guess—Rhonda would rather work with a company she knows and doesn't like than with one she can't boss around."

"You said that, not me!" Sandy laughed, but then shifted to a quieter, more serious tone. "And as for why she doesn't like Destination Dream, I'm not going to spread any rumors. Dennis has always seemed like a decent guy to me. Not a smooth talker, never one to butter anyone up, but reliable. Like I told you, I don't dig too deep. I think it's best to just stay out of her way."

"Now I know there's more to the story." Bea was about to cajole more dirt out of Sandy when an SUV rounding the bend caught their attention. "What do you think of that, Sandy? Normal wedding stuff?"

The SUV had bright lettering promoting "Hen Party: Fowl Rentals for Fun Occasions," with pictures of chickens and other barnyard birds.

"Can't say as I know," Sandy said, laughing and walking away. "I've got to get my gear set up. I'll be back with my books."

Angela spotted the poultry people and waved as she rushed over from the inn entrance.

"The birds won't be hard to carry, I hope?" Angela asked. "Barn's down that way."

"Not at all," said the chicken hand. He opened the hatch of the SUV and pulled out a large chicken-wire crate with a handle on top. "Lead the way."

Angela started toward the barn, chicken man in tow.

"Hold up, Angie," Bea said, picking up Bijou's leash. "I'm folding up my tent for now. I don't want to miss whatever it is you're going to do with those birds!"

CHAPTER 5

"Not quite as entertaining as I expected," Bea said.

Bea, Angela, and Bijou were looking at the little chicken yard Angela had set up beside the barn. Bijou pulled on the leash and sniffed curiously at the three chickens, the duck, and the fluffy white goose. The chickens took a short flight and landed a few feet away, then resumed pecking the feed Angela had spread all over the ground.

"They give kind of authentic farm feeling, though, right?" Angela said.

"Chicken coop and all," Bea said. The coop was almost a miniature of the barn. "Authentic farm feeling. That's what people want at a wedding?"

"Apparently. Should we look inside? I'm dying to see what Fiona and George—Georgina—have done with the place."

With a big breath, Angela yanked the handle of the barn's huge door. The door moved along its metal track with a scraping sound, finally opening enough for them to slip inside.

Angela gasped at the barn's transformation. "Oh my goodness, Bea. Look!"

Satiny draped fabric and strings of golden lights that looked like little Mason jars hung from the rafters. A long, rectangular table ran down the center of the barn, dressed with beautiful linens and place settings. Overflowing flower arrangements burst from big tin watering cans set on top.

"I think those fluffy flowers are peonies," Angela said. "They look magical. Gosh, it even smells like flowers in here. Must be all the roses."

At the other end of the barn, a smaller, farm-house-style table with two inviting tufted chairs stood on a platform. It was covered with waves of silky fabric and lace, placed artfully to expose a hand-carved leg. A lavish flower arrangement ran the length of the tabletop. Angela rushed over for a closer look.

"Is that for the king and queen of the prom?"

Bea cracked. "Conveniently elevated for holding court."

Bea stayed just inside the door, next to a gigantic wooden barrel that was almost as tall as she was. The cask's top was decorated with pillar candles and glass bowls filled with peach-colored roses. Next to it stood a wrought iron easel, crafted in a rustic, curly-cue style. The chalkboard it held was partially covered with a black velvet cloth. Bijou nosed around near Bea's feet.

Angela rolled her eyes. "It's called a sweetheart table, Bea. I think it's romantic."

"Sweetheart table, huh? I thought you said you didn't know anything about this wedding stuff. Someone's been doing a little research."

"Of course I've done *a little* research. We're hosting the wedding industry here, in case you hadn't noticed. It's called preparation," Angela said. "It's what professionals do."

"It's also what people with wedding fever do," Bea said.

"I don't have wedding fever! Stop saying that!"

"Calm down, girlie. It's not like I'm going to tell Aseem. At least not right away."

"Bea!"

"Just kidding."

Bijou let out a low woof and tugged her leash,

pulling Bea under the hayloft behind the easel. To prep the barn for Fiona and Georgina, Angela had hidden a wheelbarrow, farm implements, and other tools housed under the loft with two stands of velvety black pipe-and-drape. Bijou decided something behind the fabric needed exploring. Bea dropped the leash and peered under the drapery as Bijou pulled one sheet aside.

"Well, lookee here," Bea said. "Angie, looks like we picked up a squatter."

A blonde peeped sheepishly from behind the drapes. She wore high-waisted pants in a black-and-white herringbone pattern, a cotton sweater, and a lacy camisole that might have doubled as lingerie. Her thick, golden hair was pulled back in a loose braid. "Not squatting," she said. She looked around furtively and whispered, "Are you two alone?"

"George! I mean, Georgina!" Angela said, rushing over and hugging her old pal. "Why are you hiding?"

"Not hiding," Georgina said, taking a step away from Angela, and from her nook. "I… well, I was just checking on some things we stowed here, and then when you came in, it just seemed awkward to come out. I didn't want to interrupt you."

"Sure, I can see that," Angela said brightly.

Bea's skeptical expression dissolved into amusement. "Why did you ask if anyone else—" Bea started to say.

"Oh, George*ina*," Angela said. "I can't believe how you and Fiona transformed this old barn. Georgina, this is Bea, also known as Betty Snickerdoodle. Bea, this is Georgina, my college friend—"

"I get the picture. Nice to meet you, Georgina."

"You, too, Bea," Georgina said, maneuvering next to the easel. She casually reached up and flipped up the corner of the cloth that was caught on one side of the easel. The velvet now completely covered the chalkboard, obscuring a handwritten announcement that credited the design to Fiona and Georgina.

"You'll want to remove that for the photos, won't you?" Sandy Givens said, slipping through the barn door with a large camera around her neck. "Place looks great. Definitely that high-end rustic mash-up so many brides want these days. You'll want credit, won't you? And where's Fiona? She should be here for the photo op. The journalist is here, too."

A twenty-something reporter with a saucy pixie cut, tight jeans, and a tank top slipped in behind Sandy. "Hi everyone—Alexis Greene, *Wine*

Country Grapevine. Nice to see you, Bea, Angela—and you must be Georgina, right?"

"Lexie?" said Angela. "What are you—"

"Yep, Angela, you guessed it. I'm still on the fluff-and-puff beat. My latest big assignment is wine-country wedding trends."

Months before, Angela had helped Lexie save her job by teaching her how to shore up her employer's dwindling audience on a shoestring budget with social media. They'd seemed destined to become good friends, but while covering Betty-Con, Lexie unfortunately aimed her radiating sex appeal in Aseem's direction, slamming the brakes on the possibility of friendship.

"Fiona Wheaton pitched me on a story about barn weddings, farm-to-table, all that stuff. Boss thought it had good advertising potential."

The barn door behind them scraped along its track again, accompanied by a loud grunt and a demanding voice. "Georgina? I asked Tad where to find you, and he sent me here." Rhonda Butts's tall frame and hard face emerged in the opening, looming large in the late afternoon sun.

"Don't tell her I'm here!" Georgina whispered, diving under the sweetheart table, stepping on Bijou's tail on the way. The dog let out a startled yelp, and the table wobbled precariously.

"Georgina, what are you doing under there?" Rhonda barked.

"Just… fixing the linen. It was stuck under the table leg," Georgina said as she crawled out. "Is everything OK, Rhonda? Everything was fine in the ballroom when I checked a while ago."

"What the H-E-double-hockey-sticks is going on here?" Rhonda bellowed.

"Does she always do that H-E-double-hockey-sticks thing?" Bea snickered to Sandy.

"Oh, yes. She's quite pious," Sandy giggled under her breath.

Rhonda glared at Bea but ignored her comment. "Georgina, I mean it! What is all this?"

"It's just something Fiona Wheaton put together. It's… it's for some pictures she wanted for advertising. With her organic flower farm, I guess she's hoping to do more barn weddings," Georgina replied slowly. "I'm not really involved. Angela asked me for help overseeing it—to protect her property. But that's it."

"Givens, I suppose you're here taking the pictures for Fiona's ads?" Rhonda snarled. "I didn't realize you were such good friends."

"The pictures are for the media story, too," Sandy said placidly. "I could use some media exposure myself." Bea tucked her chin down to conceal her smirk, then winked at Sandy the second Rhonda looked away.

"Media story?"

"For our website," Lexie said. "I'm Alexis Greene with *Wine Country Grapevine.* I'm new to the wedding beat."

"Angela, why wasn't I told about this?" Rhonda bellowed. "You told me the event venue was the ballroom. You said nothing about this barn."

"We've never had an event in here," Angela said. "Fiona noticed a picture of the barn on our website. She asked to do a separate photo shoot. It wasn't going to interfere with your mixer, so I said yes. This little barn will only hold about fifty people, and you were interested in much larger weddings. Besides, last time I checked, I don't need your permission."

Bea looked at Angela with two enthusiastic thumbs up. "Good one, girlie!"

"So Fiona gets a media story in a brand new venue—and it doesn't even have any of those stupid Christmas trees," Rhonda huffed. "Fine. But I'll be able to book barn weddings for my fancy organic brides, too. Right?"

"We haven't decided whether we will offer *any* weddings, Rhonda," Angela said calmly. Then she blurted, "But technically, I've already promised

Fiona and Geor—Fiona and her wedding coordinator, I mean—that they can have an exclusive on this barn if we do open it up for events."

Bea guffawed and raised a fist above her head.

"I'm sorry, Rhonda, but a deal's a deal. Anyway, shouldn't you be tending to your mixer? It's starting soon, right?"

Rhonda glowered at Angela but didn't respond. "Georgina. Come. Now!" Then she turned on her heel and stormed out, marching too close to one of the chickens. It scrambled into the air with a terrified squawk, a couple of feathers floating behind it.

Bea followed Georgina as she hustled after Rhonda. "Psst. Gorgeous George, shouldn't we take the shroud off now?" She was standing by the easel, lifting one side of the cloth that concealed the chalkboard with Georgina and Fiona's names on it. "Cow's out of the barn, in more ways than one. And don't you want your name in the pictures for the website?"

"Not now! Please! She might come back," Georgina gasped as she ran to catch up with Rhonda.

"I see there's still no shortage of drama here," Lexie smirked. "But I don't have a story yet. Too bad Rhonda wasn't friendlier. I might have done a side piece on how brides can work with one of Northern California's top wedding planners."

"Yeah, I've got the perfect headline: 'Run Away, Bride!'" Bea said. She slapped her knee and doubled over guffawing.

Lexie smirked and turned to Sandy. "I still need copy. Angela, do you know where Fiona is? I won't have much of a story if I can't interview her."

"Not a clue. If I find her in the ballroom, I'll send her your way. Sandy, do you want to capture some outside shots in the meantime?"

As the four of them turned to leave, a woman appeared in shadow in the door. She wore a flowing skirt in a gauzy material and a sunny yellow cardigan tied at the waist. Her thick, shoulder-length blonde hair was pretty, pinned half-up in a messy, untamed sort of way.

"Sorry, I'm afraid I'm a bit late," she said in a charming British accent. "I'm Fiona Wheaton. Did I miss anything important?"

"You noticing a trend?" Angela giggled.

Angela and Aseem were walking the ballroom as vendors put the finishing touches on their displays. Though their romance was just a few months old, checking out wedding vendors didn't stir up any pressure or anxiety. Sometimes, now that their love story was in full bloom, Aseem felt unsure of how to navigate their business relationship, but on matters purely of the heart, he and Angela never seemed out of sync. The wedding mixer hadn't introduced any awkwardness to their relationship at all—at least not so far.

In fact, they'd shared the same bemused reaction to everything they were learning about the wedding business. There were so many categories of products and services for weddings that they'd never even heard of. And every single vendor seemed to believe their offering was the key to a perfect wedding day.

They approached a long, skirted table, where a man and a woman in white tuxedo shirts and black slacks were setting up chafing dishes and a large box with compartments for salad and condiments.

"Artful salad presentation," Angela said, admiring the pretty wood box that lent a stylish look to the ordinary metal hotel pans.

"I'd be happy to send you a link to their website. This plastic shield can be removed for a buffet.

We don't recommend that for weddings, though. All it takes is one guest's germy hand in the salad fixings to change your mind about that. I'm obsessed with hygiene. I'd imagine most caterers are," the woman said, pulling a card from one pocket of her pants and a white chef's hat from the other. "I'm Paige Brice, Sac & Back Catering."

Paige handed the card to Angela and gave the hat a shake. "Suppose I should put this on. Almost showtime. By the way, thanks for the use of your kitchen. Those local produce sources on your website were helpful, too—great product. Speaking of which," Paige said to her coworker, "Did those bags of salad greens and other veg make it to the walk-in?" The young man nodded and said he'd had a walk-through of the kitchen with Georgina and finished putting the salads together.

"Do you cater all the mixers?" Aseem asked.

"Someone always does—all of us caterers want to show off to the community. Gotta keep those referrals coming. The other vendors won't admit it," Paige added secretively, "but everyone knows food makes a wedding reception. What do people remember from weddings? How great the food was—or wasn't. Nothing creates lasting wedding memories like great food. Except maybe food poisoning," Paige chuckled.

Paige knocked on the wood salad box. "Shouldn't joke about that. Better not tempt the gods. Food poisoning's a caterer's worst nightmare. I'm lucky it's never happened to me." She knocked the box again. "I'm determined to make sure it never does."

Two good-looking DJs were starting their sound checks, one on each end of the stage. The one on the left fiddled with equipment on a podium that displayed a sign for "Get Granny Dancing by DJ Tad." DJ Tad had sandy blond hair, broad shoulders, and impossibly straight posture. The other podium promoted "The Wizard of Weddings." A striking man in his late thirties, with hazelnut-toned skin, close-cropped black hair, and a neatly trimmed beard around his mouth and chin, walked onto the stage behind it.

"Sandy told us those DJs are two of Rhonda's favorites," Angela whispered to Aseem. Two women setting up a display of chair covers waved to the DJs with big smiles. One of them blew a kiss. "I guess Rhonda's not the only one with a thing for DJs."

A third DJ stood behind a table next to the stage, keeping his head down. He rolled two trunks under the table and placed a stack of brochures and a small sign saying "Destination Dream" on top. A trim man of about fifty stood in front of the table with Rhonda. He had a hang-dog expression on his ruddy face that looked permanent.

"You got the overflow parking shuttle opportunity, Dennis," Rhonda hissed.

"Opportunity?" the man sneered. "You said my DJ could co-emcee the event in return for me providing the limo. Gas for a stretch don't grow on trees, Rhonda." He looked up at the DJ on the right-hand side of the stage and scowled, then looked back at his own DJ behind the display table. "Not to mention the hassle of bringing the DJ equipment up here—for nothing."

"You're getting to show off your ride. Why can't you be grateful for once? It's not like there aren't up-and-comers who wanted your spot."

"Rhonda, compared to me, you're an up-and-comer. I was in this business for fifteen years before you even came to town. Besides, you've given an emcee spot to Tad every month for the past year. I know he's your teacher's pet, Rhonda, but shouldn't someone else get a turn?"

"Since you're so experienced, you should be able to roll with a change of plans. Suck it up. We all have to. How was I to know the stage would be this small? The manager never told me the dimensions."

"How about a cut of the mixer fees, then? You help the caterers with food costs."

"You seem to have forgotten that business is a two-way street. You want me to play nice, you play nice."

Rhonda didn't wait for a response and turned to leave. She was startled to see Angela standing behind her, mouth agape, but strode by without acknowledging her.

Angela looked at Dennis. "Rhonda inspected this room, and she was given all the dimensions—"

"Save your breath. Not my first rodeo with Rhonda," Dennis said. "I'm Dennis Poundstone, Destination Dream Limo & DJ."

"Angela Garcia. I run the inn. I work with Bea Sickles. She's the brilliant author behind Betty Snickerdoodle."

"I'm not much of a reader. My wife loves those Snickerdoodle books, though. She's got a book club with all her church pals, and they all do."

"I wish she'd come along with you."

"She's had her fill of the wedding world. Does my bookkeeping now, thank goodness, but stays in the background. Too much drama for her taste. Sorry to say I've been at the center of some of it. Weddings are pretty, but our drama ain't. Surprised you're thinking of hosting weddings here. You having trouble making ends meet or something? I guess it's harder to run a business in the wine country than I would have guessed."

Angela stepped backward involuntarily, stepping on Aseem's foot. Her face reddened. "Nothing like that. I just heard from Rhonda about what a great opportunity—"

"No offense," Dennis interrupted. "You seem like a nice young lady. My advice is to stay far away from Rhonda. Place like this—the whole holiday gimmick you got going, it's cute—you could do a few nice weddings a year for people who like the Christmas thing, without getting involved with that wannabe mafiosa. Just make sure you audition vendors and don't let anyone you haven't hand-selected work here. Don't let anyone try to take over, because once someone like Rhonda gets her claws in—"

"Boss, got a minute?" the limo driver yelled from across the room. "I need help backing out of a tight spot."

"Gotta run. By the way, if you take my advice

and do your own weddings, take extra care in who you choose to let DJ here."

"Let me guess," Angela said. "The DJ's the most important part of a wedding reception?"

"I say what's most important depends on the taste of the couple. But one thing's for sure: a bad DJ can ruin everything."

CHAPTER 6

The mixer was underway. A line of wedding professionals waiting to check in and collect their name tags stretched down the hall and into the reception area. The vibe inside the ballroom was lively. Vendors chatted genially over Paige's snacks and drinks from the bar. The Wizard of Weddings was playing music and making occasional announcements.

Aseem eventually made his way to the front of the line. "Do these mixers always draw such a crowd?"

"Not like this," the woman checking him in said. "A new venue in Napa is a huge deal. Rhonda didn't have to twist our arms."

Aseem made his way through the crowd to the

perimeter of the ballroom. He entertained himself while he waited for Angela by politely checking out the few tables they hadn't visited together.

Fiona's table was still unattended and empty, except for a small, lonely looking sign. Aseem leaned over and smiled as he read it. It said "KEEP CALM AND MIX ON" in a familiar white typeface on a bright red background. Underneath, in pretty script, Fiona had written, "If I'm not here, take a walk around the back of this lovely inn and see me in the barn."

Aseem looked up and saw a man in his early fifties hurrying toward him. His salt-and-pepper hair was disheveled. "Always running late, I'm afraid," he said. He scooted behind the table and extended a hand. "I'm Gary."

Aseem introduced himself. He caught himself staring at Gary's chest, but not before Gary did. "Sorry, it's just—"

Gary looked down at his branded button-down shirt, the peach color of which matched the color of the cloth on the display table. "Can't be spilled coffee—I haven't had any," he laughed. "Is it the name on the shirt? Playfair Petals—it's the name of Fiona's new farm in Playfair Pines.

"Oh! I get it!" Gary finally realized his shirt was on inside out. Then he leaned over the table toward Aseem and made a motion with his elbow like he was nudging him in the ribs. "Fee and I couldn't resist christening the room, if you know what I mean."

Aseem squinted and shifted his weight.

"Sorry! I know, awkward. I may have been to a half-dozen black-tie dinners at the governor's mansion, but I guess I still don't really know how to behave. Fee says I'll always be a teenage geek in a man's body."

"So you and Fiona, I mean Fee, you're—"

"Married almost twenty years now. Were you thinking I was trying to sleep my way to the top? Fee would love that idea. I don't usually come to these things, but who doesn't jump at an excuse for a night in the wine country? The rooms are comfortable, too. Especially the beds. The Christmas thing's a little disorienting at first, but we found a way to ignore it."

Gary repeated his nudge-nudge gesture and winked lasciviously at Aseem, who cringed again.

"What's your connection to the mixer? No offense, but you don't look like a wedding vendor."

Aseem smiled. "I work for the inn. I handle all the tech and a lot of the operations stuff. I always wanted to be part of a startup. It's not Silicon Valley, but thanks to Angela, I'm getting a startup experience of sorts. I guess you could say I'm her lieutenant."

"Angela's the manager of the inn, right?"

"She's the president of Betty Snickerdoodle, Inc. The inn, the books, BettyCon—all of it."

"Nice. Ambitious. Fee's impressed with her. I hear she's quite a looker, too."

"Hey, that's my girlfriend you're talking about," Aseem grinned.

"Oops! Awkward Gary strikes again. How do you two manage that? Is it uncomfortable dating the boss?"

"It's… it's not always easy. What's it like for you and Fiona? You've been together for a long time now. Have you worked in her company the whole time?"

"I don't work in Fee's company," Gary said, chuckling. "We did work together in my company before we were married—years ago, back when it was a startup. Fee worked in marketing and was fantastic at it. But when we started to have some success, the business took up most of my time, and Fee started to feel like she was playing second fiddle. She'd always wanted to build something of her own. The flower business was her dream. I wanted to help her—share what I'd learned from my own startup. But I found that was touchy. I wasn't always sure if she wanted to hear my opinions, especially when they differed from hers."

Aseem smiled and nodded.

"Besides, what do I know about flowers?" Gary laughed. "If she'd needed advice on scaling up a server farm, I'd have been her guy. Flower farms, not so much. I learned early to avoid too many comments from the peanut gallery, even when I thought she was making mistakes. Heck, sometimes even if she asked for my opinion—let's just say I learned it might be better to hold back."

Aseem's eyes widened. "Did you ever feel like... like if she asks you a question, there's a right answer, but you don't know what it is?"

"Oh, yeah. The thing is, everything I said carried too much weight. If I disagreed, she sometimes felt like I was panning her ideas."

"And if you agreed, you were just humoring her?"

Gary laughed. "Yep. The most important thing I realized was this: even though her business was smaller than mine—let's face it, a lot smaller—I had to respect it, just like my own."

"I can understand Fiona wanting to make her own mark. I've got ideas for my own apps. I hope I can make time for both my work at the inn and my app projects, so I try to work on them on the side—" Aseem paused and his jaw dropped, as if he'd realized something important.

The chocolatier at the next table interrupted them. "Can I interest either of you in a truffle? They're going fast."

"I wish I could," Gary said, patting his tummy. "I'm on this weird diet. It's called bio-hacking."

"How could I not have recognized—" Aseem stammered, "you're *Gary Wheaton*. You've… you've been a hero of mine for years. I mean, you're probably a hero to everyone in tech. Your infrastructure software changed everything from scalability to security. And now artificial intelligence—"

"Aw shucks. Here I was trying to be incognito. If I can't go unnoticed at a wedding mixer, where can I?"

Aseem started to apologize, but Gary laughed reassuringly. "Just kidding. As long as you don't lecture me on how technology is ruining the world, I'm happy to know you. Maybe I can even help you with those app ideas. I'm investing in startups now." He reached into both pockets and eventually found a business card that looked like it had been through the wash. "A little lint won't hurt you, and the contact info's right. Now you know why Fee says she can't take me anywhere.

Speaking of Fee, here she comes—not a moment too soon. She can take over the table and I can go drain the ol' dragon."

Just your average awkward billionaire tech hero, thought Aseem.

He smiled at the card like he was dreaming, then tucked it into his wallet with extra care, as if it were a bit of an ancient scroll. When he looked up Fiona was there, extending her alabaster hand toward him and introducing herself with a smile.

AN HOUR INTO THE MIXER, DJ TAD HAD TAKEN over as emcee and was leaning casually against his podium. Bea approached the stage and beckoned him toward her. He smiled and crouched at the edge of the stage to speak with her. Angela watched him shake his head and shrug. Then Bea turned away from the stage, and Angela could see her snap her fingers and mouth "nuts."

"Bea!" Angela called to her, waving her over. "Everything OK?"

"Yeah. I told him I was old enough to be a great-granny and I wanted to do a little dancing. DJ Tad said it's not appropriate while people are networking and that Georgina was about to make an announcement. Too bad. I asked him to play 'Help Me, Rhonda' as a tribute to their fearless leader. I wanted to see if anyone would sing along —or whether they'd laugh. Get it, Angie? 'Help Me, Rhonda'?" Bea chuckled.

Angela didn't respond. She'd noticed Georgina making her way from the kitchen entrance to the stage, looking pale and tense. Once Georgina reached the stage, DJ Tad adjusted the microphone and guided her by her elbow to the podium, smiling sweetly at her. Before stepping away, Tad gave her shoulders a quick squeeze as she moved behind the microphone, as if trying to help her relax. Georgina tapped the top of the microphone nervously.

"This thing on?" Georgina laughed uneasily. "Old joke, I know.

Angela scanned the room and turned back to Bea. "Does it seem like a lot of people have left already?"

"Now that you mention it," Bea said, "it seems a lot less crowded all of a sudden."

"Look at those display tables, too. They're still set up, but no one's minding them."

Georgina forged on with her announcements. "As you all know, at this point in the mixer Rhonda introduces all the vendors who made our event possible. But Rhonda texted me that she had to leave. She didn't say why… but I'm sure everything's fine. I guess you're stuck with me, though." She leaned toward the microphone and another jittery laugh slipped out, and the microphone sent whiny feedback through the speakers. "Sorry!" she said, jerking her head back from the microphone. "OK, here we go."

Angela cringed with sympathy for her poor friend. Then she and Bea noticed Sandy Givens making fast strides toward the door, looking miserable. "Don't tell me you're missing Rhonda," Bea cackled as Sandy hurried past.

"Nothing like that," Sandy said, forcing a smile. Her face looked pale. "I'm feeling queasy all of a sudden. I'm heading back to my room until it passes. I hope it's just the power of suggestion. I was talking to Dennis Poundstone a couple of minutes ago, and he rushed off—sick to his stomach. Don't worry, though. I'm still looking forward to coffee with you in the morning."

"Good—I want the rest of the gossip!" said Bea. "Bring your books so I can sign them."

"Feel better, Sandy," Angela said.

Georgina continued to stumble stiffly through her talk, noticing too late that many of the vendors she'd planned to introduce were not at their tables and having to awkwardly correct herself.

"That's got to be weird, right? Didn't those vendors set their tables up just for this moment in the spotlight?" Angela said. "Sandy and Dennis were both feeling ill, too—do you think there's a bug going around?"

A loud crash interrupted Georgina and startled Bea, Angela, and everyone else in the room. The chocolatier was rushing unsteadily toward one of the French doors that led onto the deck. In her haste, she'd bashed into her display table, knocking it over. She ignored the mess and the noise and kept hurrying to the door, shoving it open with such force that it slammed against the wall. Everyone in the room watched in horror as she wobbled desperately toward the stairs that led down to the grounds, barely unable to reach them before a torrent of orange and green vomit splattered onto the deck.

"Good thing Rhonda said she's taking care of everything," Bea cracked. "Looks like your old pal Georgie Girl isn't in the pink, either." On the stage, Georgina looked pale and lost as she tried to finish her announcements.

"Maybe that's stage fright, though," Angela

said. "I bet Rhonda never even gave her a turn at the microphone."

"Pardon me!" shouted one of the linen vendors, rushing for the door with her hand over her mouth.

"Oh dear," Angela said.

"Oh dear, indeed," Bea said, stepping aside as Dennis's DJ, an elderly harpist, and one of the videographers bolted past them for the exit looking green. "I hope Rhonda's plan included a haz-mat crew!"

CHAPTER 7

"Back in the day, this might have been the sign of a good party," Bea said. She laughed and chucked Angela on the shoulder with her fist. But Angela would not be cheered up. Her big, brown eyes were watering, tears threatening to fall from her long lashes.

The sun was already blazing bright and warm, though it had only just come up. Angela had already been out of bed for nearly two hours.

"In no way could this be considered a good morning, Bea. I'm just glad Georgina woke me so I could check on all the guests. What if Georgina hadn't heard Dennis thrashing against the wall? What if no one had discovered he'd had a seizure?"

From Bea's little pull-down bench on the side of the inn, they watched—Angela in the lightweight sweats and t-shirt she wore to bed, Bea in her nightie and a bathrobe, her slippers barely touching the ground—as EMTs closed the doors on an ambulance. Angela and Bea had heard Sandy moaning softly as the EMTs lifted her on a gurney into the back. Another ambulance had already driven off with its lights flashing, carrying Dennis Poundstone. Two more were parked with their doors open, ready for passengers. The EMTs were making rounds inside the inn, checking on the sickest guests to determine if anyone else needed to go to the hospital. A few moments later, one EMT jogged out of the inn and pulled the gurney down from one of the ambulances. "We've got one more fainter who should be checked at the ER," he told Angela and Bea. "She's got a heart condition and we're concerned about her level of dehydration."

Georgina walked toward Bea and Angela. Already dressed for the day, Georgina nervously tugged her sleeves down as she walked, a serious expression on her face. As she stood in front of them and began to speak, she tucked her hands into her pants pockets.

"It looks bad, I know. But there is good news,

Angela. Most of the other cases were mild. The EMTs told me that Sandy and Dennis should make a full recovery. It was probably dehydration from all the—you know—all the vomiting, but with a seizure and a fainting spell, it's smart to get them to the hospital. It seems likely they'll make a full recovery."

Angela opened her mouth to respond, but only managed a whisper. "The EMTs just said they're worried another of the sick guests has a heart condition."

Georgina paused for a moment. "I'm sure… I'm sure everyone will be fine, Angela. But I have to tell you, the health department will be here later this morning. I'm sorry, I had to call them. It's standard event procedure with food-borne illness. I know you're probably worried it will blow back on your business."

"Aren't you worried it will blow back on you?" Bea said. "Or rather, you and Rhonda? Your caterers brought the food."

"We've never had a problem at any other location. Paige and her crew have catered nearly a thousand weddings and events without an issue. The difference this time is they had to rely on your walk-in refrigerator and kitchen. Maybe the chiller's temperature control malfunctioned? That's the kind of thing the inspector checks."

Angela shook her head. "That doesn't make sense. The walk-in is practically new. I personally worked with the vendor and the chef to set everything up precisely to code."

"Even new equipment can malfunction. I didn't see a temperature alarm near the walk-in."

"It's wireless and very small. I'll have to check with Aseem, but I can't imagine it wasn't working."

"Possibly a problem with your local produce suppliers, then? Don't worry. We'll get to the bottom of it." Georgina looked sympathetically at Angela. "I've contacted everyone who attended last night. Every person who got ill ate at the mixer last night, and none of them had any other foods in common within twenty-four hours of the event. Seems pretty clear it was something they ate here at the inn. I'll forward their contacts to you, in case you or the inspector need to follow up. I told the people who aren't feeling well enough to leave that I'd ask if they could stay until this evening. Is it OK to leave a few cars parked at Heavenly West for today?"

Angela nodded. "Connie—the owner—is out of town."

"I've got to get back to Sacramento. I'm helping Rhonda with that wedding in Capitol Park tomorrow. You still planning to take her up on her—I mean, our—invitation to observe?"

"Doubtful," Angela said. "Hard to imagine we'll go ahead with weddings here now, so there's not much need to learn more."

"You don't have to decide now, do you, Angie?" Bea said.

Angela squinted at Bea. "I suppose not. OK if I text you in the morning, Georgina?"

"No need. Just show up if you're interested. Should be one of our loveliest. The roses are in full bloom. As long as you stay discreet, you can observe all you want. With these public garden weddings, uninvited observers are always expected. Of course, I'll try to show you as many ins-and-outs of running a wedding as I can."

"Thanks for all the help, Georgina. I appreciate it. You're a real friend."

"True friendship never ends, right? I almost forgot," Georgina said as she walked away, "the state health inspector's name is Eric Delvecchio. He'll be here later this morning. I probably don't have to tell you to be courteous. Give him what he needs. Don't try to fight it. There's still a chance your inn can bounce back. Chin up!"

Angela sighed and stood up from the bench. "Shaping up to be a fun day, wouldn't you say? Massive disaster and we aren't even out of our PJs. I'm going to take a shower and get a cup of coffee. Would you like one? Maybe I'll drive downtown and get a fancy iced coffee."

"You know I would never refuse that, Angie."

"Sounds like a plan. But Bea, there's something I don't get. You weren't thrilled about the wedding mixer in the first place. Why are you so keen on observing that wedding tomorrow?"

"No reason," Bea said. "Maybe I just thought you should indulge your wedding fever."

Angela sighed and put her face in her hands. "Bea, really, now is not the time."

"Just kidding, trying to cheer you up a little, girlie. Listen, a road trip might be fun. The weather's great and everything's in bloom. If we have time, we could visit your mom—or take a side trip to Thunder Valley for a few hands of poker."

"A road trip might be fun. But why do I think you're up to something?" Tiny crinkles formed near Angela's eyes. "As long as we can get everything done with the health inspector today, we can go, provided I can get someone to keep an eye on the dogs until Connie comes back tomorrow afternoon. We can stop for a slice at that pizza place you love on I-80, too."

"Sounds perf, girlie. I can taste the pepperoni already." Bea leaned back against the inn. "I think I'll enjoy a little sun here while you get our coffee."

Angela started to head back to her suite, but something caught her eye and she slumped back down on the bench with Bea, desperate to avoid running into one of the last people she wanted to see at that moment.

"It's Lexie!" she whispered at Bea. "What on earth is she doing here?"

Lexie was walking out of the inn with DJ Tad. She was waving him off as he headed toward the parking area, but he wasn't done talking. "Like I said, I only had the salad, and Georgina did, too. We're both fine, so that may not have been the culprit. If you need anything else from me—or anything for your wedding story—just send me a text."

"I will," Lexie called after him. Despite Angela's best effort to be inconspicuous, Lexie spotted her and Bea right away. Once she saw Tad hopping into the cab of his truck, Lexie headed toward the bench. "That guy's got no shortage of self-esteem. You should have heard him go on about how careful he has to be about his diet to protect his voice."

"I'm more curious how he has so much energy this morning," Bea said. "I thought I heard those DJs wheeling their gear out in the wee hours last night. In between, you know, all the sounds of people vomiting."

"I suspect that most DJs are night owls—"

"Fascinating, Lexie," Angela said. "But not as fascinating as how you just happen to be here at this hour. The owls have gone to bed and the morning birds aren't even awake."

"Angela, you sound nervous. But please don't be. I'm not trying to sabotage—"

"Aren't you here doing a story?"

"I got an anonymous tip that something happened that might affect my wedding story—naturally, I was curious. They didn't say what it was, but I was up early and didn't have anything better to do on this beautiful morning. So I thought I'd come over and interview a few more wedding people. Angela, you know our little publication can't afford to lose your support. I'm not in the business of hurting our biggest advertisers—"

Angela snorted. "Even I am not that gullible. Since when are you going to miss out on a scoop, even if—no, especially if—it capitalizes on someone's misfortune? If you're done talking to wedding people—no, whether you're done or not—I want you off the property. I mean it, Lexie. Go. Now."

Angela got up from the bench and headed back into the inn to her suite.

Lexie looked at Bea with a smile both wry and sheepish. "I guess that's my cue to leave," she said with a carefree shrug.

"Haha, Hot Pants, you're not fooling anybody. We both know you're lying."

"Maybe I'm fibbing a little," Lexie said as she walked away. "But I'm telling the truth about not wanting to hurt Angela or your inn. I'm not going to be bullied out of a story, though, even if you kick me off the property."

As she walked away from Bea, Lexie took her phone out of her pocket. She held it up and tracked the path of the ambulance that was driving off with Sandy Givens in the back, then got into her small sedan. She drove it from the parking lot onto the street and parked on the curb, then got out of the driver's side carrying a laptop. She sat on the trunk lid with the computer and waved at Bea.

"Freedom of the Press. America's greatest tradition," she shouted at Bea.

"Suit yourself, Hot Pants," Bea shouted back. "But I think you're barking up the wrong tree."

Lexie curled her hands in front of her coyly and said, "Woof! Just kidding. I know it's tough to trust a reporter, but in this case, you can. You really can."

CHAPTER 8

Standing stiffly in the reception area, Eric Delvecchio looked to Angela like an unusually attractive man trying his hardest to look like a dork.

She couldn't be sure, since the waistband was hidden under his blue blazer and white Oxford-cloth shirt, but Angela guessed Eric's plaid pants were expensive golf slacks—the ironic millennial variety, hiked up to look nerdy. His thick-framed, plain black glasses could be fake. His hair was messy, with bangs flopping down onto the flawless, olive-toned skin of his forehead, but it looked to Angela like the hand-crafted messiness women often aim for. Eric carried his clipboard close to his body, almost protectively.

The biggest hint was the stubble, though.

Designer whiskers, thought Angela. *Definitely not the look of a real nerd.*

Of course, Angela would never have said a word about the food safety inspector's costumed appearance. She assumed that he wanted to fit in, to be taken seriously. *That can be hard when you're too pretty,* she thought charitably. Though she had no intention of outing him, guessing at his secret made her relax just a little. Eric Delvecchio looked to be about her age. Angela, of all people, could relate to an ambitious young professional simply trying to do a good job and make his mark in the world.

"I'm Angela Garcia," she said, extending a hand. "Of course, the safety of our guests is top priority for everyone here at the inn. I'll show you whatever you need to see. My technology director will join us in a moment." She pulled out her phone and texted Aseem. "He'll be able to answer any questions you have about the fridge alarm."

Minutes later, the three of them were heading from the lobby toward the kitchen when Bea intercepted them. She was conspicuously using her cane, as she always did when she wanted to be sure she'd be treated like a sweet little old lady.

"Hold up, Angie dear," Bea called out in a

creaky voice. She was shuffling slowly, leaning over her cane. "Rheumatism acting up this morning. Oh my goodness, Angie, would you please carry this iced coffee for me? I'm afraid it's just too heavy. Thank you so much for getting it for me." Bea was swimming in one of her favorite oversized track suits, this one in a color-block design in four eye-searing day-glo colors.

Angela's right eyebrow climbed halfway to her hairline. Aseem turned his face away from Eric and suppressed a smirk.

"I'm Bea," Bea said, extending her free hand limply toward Eric's. "Did you say your name was Clark?"

"Eric. Eric Delvecchio."

"Oh my, I don't know where I got Clark from," Bea said, shaking her head. "Old noggin not working its best today, I guess. All the stress about your visit and all."

"And the ill people—right, Bea?" Angela added quickly. "We're both worried, of course, that everyone will be all right. Nothing like this has ever happened here."

"Yes, of course, Angie dear. Now Clark—I mean, Eric—you wouldn't mind showing us some identification, would you?"

"Certainly, I apologize," Eric said. He reached into his pocket for a plastic badge holder with an ID card tucked inside. He used the metal clip at the top to attach it to his lapel.

Bea leaned in to within an inch of his chest. "Bend down, please. I can't see it." Eric complied, looking uncomfortable. "There, that's better. Everything seems to be in order." Bea tapped on the badge with her crooked finger. "Thank you. Shall we proceed?"

Angela sighed. "Shall we head to the kitchen?"

"Seems quite clean," Eric said, surveying the spotless floors and the gleaming metal of the workspace and appliances. "So far, so good." He marked a dramatic check on his clipboard. Angela peered discreetly over his bicep, hoping to notice anything else he might have written.

Eric used the foot pedal to the lid of the round trash bin that stood against the wall. The bin's exterior was immaculate, like new. Angela stood beside the inspector as he picked out one of four large plastic salad sacks that were resting on top of the trash. They were branded "Perfection Produce."

"Is this a local vendor?"

"Yes," Angela replied. "It's one of the companies I list on our website as a local partner. Many restaurants nearby use them. I believe the wedding caterers contacted them for fresh produce they didn't want to transport from Sacramento. You do know that the caterers brought food of their own as well, I assume?"

"I see." Eric ignored the question and dropped the bag in the bin and let the lid fall into place. He turned toward the large refrigerator on the side wall. "Let's take a look at the walk-in."

"Don't you want one of those bags as a sample?" Angela said. "For your lab?" She stepped toward the pedal to reopen the lid. As she did, she noticed the edge of a filmy, plain plastic bag that had fallen behind the barrel. Worried it would undermine the kitchen's image of pristine cleanliness, she tucked the edge in with her toe, then stepped on the pedal. She picked up the Perfection Produce bag that was on top of the trash and passed it to Eric. "Here you go."

He nodded, then took the bag and folded it into a flat square, which he tucked underneath the pages on his clipboard. "Thanks."

Eric turned to the huge refrigerator. He scrutinized the exterior of the door, leaning in close and cocking his head to view the edges. "Seals and hinges look tight. Do you have a temperature monitor?"

"Right here," Aseem piped up. He pointed to the small electronic device in a bracket on the wall next to the door, tucked almost invisibly behind a shelving unit.

"Cadav-ex?" Angela said. "As in *cadaver*?"

"It's designed for morgues. Bit of a genius hack, if I say so myself," Aseem said. "Similar technology to what restaurants use, just cheaper. Even more than restaurants, morgues don't want the produce warming up."

Bea unleashed a cackle and punched Aseem on the bicep. "Good one, handsome!"

"Perfectly acceptable. Any type of monitor is fine, as long as it tracks the temperature and alerts you when it's out of range," Eric said matter-of-factly, pulling the unit from its rack.

"It tracks continuously, and alerts me via this app if the temperature rises more than a couple of degrees," Aseem said, showing Eric his phone.

"Very nice. Unfortunately, I doubt this unit is working."

"What do you mean?" Angela said.

Eric turned the little gadget around to show the three of them the underside. The plastic cover that should have protected the battery chamber was missing, as was the battery.

Angela and Aseem looked at each other, confused. "Angel, you know I put the battery in it myself months ago."

"I know you did."

"I'm going to have to make note of this in my report," Eric said, making a forceful jot on his clipboard.

"But Eric," Angela said, "just because the alarm battery was missing doesn't mean the temperature was improper in here. It feels quite cold right now. And as you said, all the seals look fine."

"Rules are rules. But let's continue and see how the rest of the inspection goes. When we're done, I may have a solution for you that could save you some trouble with my bosses."

"Really," said Bea suspiciously. But she caught herself and immediately reverted to sweet old lady mode. "Oh Eric, it would be so kind of you to help us out." Behind Eric's back, Angela grinned and rolled her eyes.

Eric pulled open the door of the walk-in. As Angela followed him in, she noticed items she hadn't seen before on shelf space that had been set aside for the caterers. There were two half-gallon containers of heavy cream, a half-sized hotel pan with its flat lid partially ajar (Angela could see it still held some chicken wings), a jar with iced green tea marked "DJ Juice," and the thing that caught Angela's attention: dozens of scrumptious-looking desserts in shot glasses, arranged neatly on sheet trays.

"I wonder what those are," Angela said. "They must have been meant for the mixer."

"Looks like mousse," said Aseem. "Chocolate, butterscotch, strawberry—yum."

"Maybe somebody was whipping cream to garnish them," Angela said. "But what's the mixing bowl doing in here?" The bowl was the eighty-quart component of an old industrial mixer the inn had inherited when the owner of a neighboring bakery retired and closed up shop. The bowl was on its battered, custom-built wooden dolly. Angela poked her head out of the walk-in to confirm the mixer itself was where it belonged. She spotted the edge of its enameled foot peeking out from its nook in the far corner of the kitchen.

Bea was standing closest to the mixing bowl. "I think you're right, Angie. There's a little cream still in the bowl." Bea looked cautiously at Eric. His back was to her, and he was inspecting the trays full of miniature mousses with deep interest. Angela saw Bea bend down and pick something off the floor and put it in one of the pockets of her garish track suit. Then Bea carefully positioned her cane, as if covering something on the side of the bowl.

"Don't see a use-by label here," Eric said officiously. "I'm afraid that's another violation for my report."

"But those were clearly intended for the mixer," Angela said, examining the tray more closely. "They would have been brought to be served within a couple of hours. Look at the cards on the trays—'Bride's Tiers Wedding Cakes and Desserts.' Rhonda must have arranged them for the mixer last night."

"Like I said, rules are rules. I don't make them, I just enforce them," Eric said smugly.

Angela's sympathy for hardworking Eric evaporated. She grimaced as she watched him write forcefully on his clipboard again, the pen making a scraping sound as he repeatedly underlined one of his notes. Her nose crinkled as he dotted an i with a loud flourish.

"Anything else you need to see, Eric? Perhaps we're done here?" She stood by the door, positioning herself to close it behind the group.

"Angel, if you don't mind, I'll have one or two of these for the road," Aseem said, grabbing one of the little jars of mousse. "No breakfast this morning—"

"No!" cried Bea. Angela and Aseem stared at her with alarm. Bea resumed her elderly innocent routine. "I am sure those have eggs in them, Aseem dear. Aren't you allergic?"

Aseem started to say no, but Angela interrupted him while also putting a gentle elbow to his ribs. "Of course mousse has eggs in it, darling." She took the jar from him and returned it to the tray. "Thank you, Bea. That was a close one." Aseem looked at her with a furrowed brow. As soon as Eric turned away, Angela mouthed, "Trust Bea."

"I think we're done here," Eric said briskly. "Angela, if you're interested in the adjustment I mentioned that can get you back into compliance immediately, I'll just go grab something out of my car."

Angela nodded, and she, Bea, and Aseem followed Eric as he strode through the reception area to the parking lot. They watched from the front doors as he tossed the clipboard onto the back seat of his boxy old off-road vehicle, then reached across to the front passenger seat to grab something. He shut the door and walked back toward the entrance.

"This would be the perfect time for him to break into a run, rip open his shirt, and reveal the bright red S on his chest," Bea chortled.

"That's why you were calling him 'Clark'—as in Clark Kent," laughed Aseem.

"Yes, but in his case, the S would stand for Superscam."

Aseem laughed and looked at Angela, expecting her to do the same. But Angela's gaze was fixed beyond the inspector on the small car parked on the road in front of the inn—and the annoying woman perched on its trunk.

"What's Lexie still doing here? I told her to leave."

"Technically, we can't tell her not to park on the road," Bea said. Angela ignored Bea and kept glaring at Lexie, who finally noticed and waved cheerfully. Angela sniffed with irritation.

"Here it is," Eric said. He was holding a small box with a refrigerator temperature monitor. "If you buy it from me and install it today, I won't have to write you up. Here's the price," he added, pointing to a handwritten figure on a sticker on the corner of the box.

"That's twenty times what I paid for ours,"

scoffed Aseem. "Why don't you just give us the battery out of the box?"

"I could do that, but your inn would still be on probation, and I'd still have to submit my report." Eric then quoted a price for the battery that would easily fill the gas tank of a large truck.

"I just remembered I have a spare battery in my suite, so I don't think we'll be in need of yours. But we thank you."

Angela started to object, but Bea interrupted her. "Thank you very much, Mr. Delvecchio," she said, once more adopting a mild, grandmotherly tone. "I'm sure you are anxious to head back to your office. Sacramento, right? The state health department? My goodness, the traffic running through our capital city to Tahoe starts earlier and earlier. Surely you'll want to avoid that."

Eric nodded stiffly and headed out to his car.

"Thank you, Eric. I mean, Mr. Delvecchio," Angela called after him. "We'll take a picture of our monitor with its new battery and send it to you. Perhaps you can include it in your report?"

"If you like. No promises."

"Are you two sure we shouldn't have spent that money? Who knows how hard it will be to get off probation," Angela fretted. She stood at the door and watched as Eric Delvecchio drove away

—and watched Lexie position herself by the entrance to the inn and snap pictures of the inspector as he drove past her onto the road. "Great! Now look what miss meddling cub reporter is up to."

"Trust me, girlie," Bea said. Her posture had returned to its almost-upright norm, and her voice had shed its faux sweetness. "I can't say for sure about Lexie, but I definitely don't think you have to worry about Eric."

But Angela was already out the door, on the march to give Lexie another piece of her mind.

"WHY CAN'T WE BE FRIENDS, ANGELA? MORE TO the point, why won't you believe me when I tell you I won't write anything to hurt you, Bea, or the inn?"

Lexie let her hands fall open, as if she were trying to explain the simplest, most obvious concept in the world. She looked completely relaxed, sitting cross-legged on the trunk of her car. Angela would have sworn Lexie was smirking.

"Gee, Lexie, could it be because *I just saw you* taking pictures of that health inspector? Or because you refused to leave the property when I asked you to? Or the fact that you're always desperate for a click-bait story?"

Angela was pacing in the road in front of Lexie, working up a head of angry steam. "Oh, and how about your track record as a 'friend'?" Angela scoffed and punctuated the last word with air quotes. "What do you think? Pretty good list of reasons, right? I can come up with more."

"Fair enough," Lexie laughed, her unshakable confidence getting right under Angela's skin. "But let me try to explain why you should trust me. We're on the same side, I promise.

"First, I admit I lied to you earlier—a little. The anonymous tip mentioned an outbreak of food-borne illness related to last night's event, and said it looked serious. And that a state health inspector had already been called, and would be showing up later this morning."

"And then you rushed over for the story? So far, I'm not seeing how this explains why I should trust you."

"I'm getting there. Did I ever tell you about my parents' cheese business?"

"No." Angela said curtly.

"Trust me—it's related. My parents are hippies. They've been more or less frozen in time since the 1960s. They moved up to Humboldt County before I was born, with big dreams of natural living. They found a little patch where they could grow vegetables and raise some chickens. Other hippie farmers were starting to grow pot—that might have been easier, but they didn't want to go that way. So they sold their extra veggies and eggs to those folks for cash to buy the things they needed. It wasn't an easy life, but it was apparently happy. Just what they hoped for, or so they tell me.

"Then by accident, they wound up with a few goats. A neighbor passed away and left his little herd to my parents. My mother had gotten into French cooking by then, watching all those Julia Child shows on a little black-and-white TV. She'd pick up the cookbooks at used bookstores whenever she could find them. And, naturally, she started learning about *le fromage.*" Lexie adopted an affected French accent and waved her hand above her head for comic effect.

Angela sighed. "Lexie, is there a point—"

"At first, the goats were like pets. My parents milked them, of course, but just for our family. Then the little herd started to grow, and so did my mom's knowledge of cheese. She got the idea of chèvre—the French-style goats' milk cheese. This was in the early 1980s, mind you—before snobby cheese was such a thing.

"Long story short—"

Angela sighed. "If only it were short—"

"Long story short, my parents became artisanal cheese pioneers. The early years were lean, but eventually they had a growing business. They started employing a few people, investing profits back into the company. Fast-forward more than a decade to my teenage years, and restaurants and specialty stores grabbed all the cheese as fast as my parents could produce it. They were getting write-ups in food magazines. My parents were still so naïve and idealistic, their big fear was that they were becoming 'the man.' What they should have worried about was jealous neighbors. Somebody sabotaged their business, and they almost lost everything."

Angela's expression softened a little. "I'm starting to see your point."

"I won't bore you with the details of who or how. But I'll tell you the line I got from that anonymous tipster reminded me of how the scam on my parents went down."

"How so?"

"For starters, *real* food safety inspectors don't let people know when they're coming. It's harder for them to catch you screwing up if you have time to prepare for them. And they're local—they don't come from Sacramento."

"Makes sense."

"Then there's the matter of the timing. Did you know that most food-borne illness takes at least twelve to twenty-four hours to incubate? Sometimes even a couple of days?"

"People at the mixer got ill within an hour or two of eating. You're saying that makes it unlikely they had food poisoning."

"Right. Probably not food poisoning, but it still could be—"

Angela gasped.

"You guessed it. Regular old-fashioned *poisoning*. Somebody could have tampered with the food at your event—just like my parents' cheese."

"Why would someone sabotage the inn, though? I don't think we have any enemies."

"My parents didn't think so either," Lexie said, grinning. "But it's possible the inn was collateral damage. Maybe someone wanted to sabotage the mixer. Or maybe someone just wanted to poison one of the guests. That's the mystery you'll need to figure out to clear the inn's reputation. Just thought you might like a little help, since I doubt you'll get any from the police—"

"Oh my gosh—I have to go," Angela said, running back to the inn.

"So does this mean we're friends now?"

"No!" shouted Angela. "OK, maybe!"

Angela jogged through the inn's front doors and headed straight back to the kitchen. She got there just in time—the housekeeper was just about to empty the trash.

"One second, please," she said breathlessly. "Let me have a look before you tie that bag."

The housekeeper stepped back and Angela stepped on the pedal to open the lid again. The three salad bags were still on top. Angela found one that still had some bits of lettuce in it, then started to look underneath it for other evidence. She squinted and squeezed her nose shut. "I need gloves… or something."

She spotted a long set of tongs—almost two feet long. "That'll do." She grabbed it and used it to poke around in the trash. Underneath it she found mostly empty containers from other produce. She pulled one out. *Should I save these? Could there be traces of poison?*

She put a plastic container that had held cherry tomatoes next to the salad bag on the prep table and resumed poking at the refuse. Then she turned to the housekeeper.

"You know what? I think we need to keep this trash for a couple of days. I'm going to tie it up and put it in the walk-in so nothing rots." Then she asked the housekeeper to go to the front desk for a sticky note, to label the bag "do not discard."

After she tied the bag, she grabbed a clean one and dropped the full bag inside it. "There. Just to keep things clean." She left the salad bag and tomato container out. She planned to look those vendors up online and contact them.

She turned to stash the trash in the walk-in and noticed something at her feet: the edge of the thin plastic bag she'd pushed out of sight. *Shoot. And I've already closed up the trash!*

As she picked it up, she noticed something: a few little leaves and bits of stem remained. They looked like designer salad fodder.

Baby greens, I think they call them. But are you innocent as a baby? She decided she'd look for pictures of different types of baby greens online.

She opened the door of the walk-in and found a solitary spot on the floor to stow the bag. Then as she turned to leave, she noticed the mixer bowl, remembering the feeling she'd had that Bea was concealing something from Eric.

Angela leaned down and examined the bowl. "Oh my gosh!" She took her cell phone from her pocket and took pictures of what she found. No wonder Bea hadn't wanted Aseem to eat the mousse.

She rolled the heavy bowl on its dolly out of the cooler to the kitchen's huge sink, and with a massive effort, heaved it into the metal basin. She let the water run until it was steaming.

I'd better get this good and clean before anyone uses it.

CHAPTER 9

"Lucky me. I scored shotgun!" Bea said, reaching up and climbing with considerable effort into the passenger seat of Angela's compact SUV. "By the way, you look nice."

"Thanks. And since when do you not get shotgun?" Angela said, laughing. Hoping to blend in with the wedding guests, she'd substituted a linen skirt, yellow top, strappy sandals, and dangling pearl earrings for her usual snappy combination of dark jeans and a crisp white blouse. She'd added a bit of eye makeup, too, and her hair was swept up in a topknot.

"Haven't you heard? Gratitude is the key to happiness. Where's your handsome boyfriend?"

"Aseem's hanging out with friends down in Silicon Valley," Angela said. She buckled herself in behind the wheel and put the key in the ignition. "Tech buddies. I'm guessing it will be a day and night of gaming."

"Can't blame him for coming up with an excuse to skip today's adventure. A sixty-mile drive for Wedding Planning 101 isn't the average young man's top pick for Saturday fun."

"Actually, he made the plans before I told him about our road trip. Besides, he says he'll be excited to learn about planning a wedding, once the time is right."

"Oh boy," Bea said, her eyes twinkling. "He knows."

"Knows what?"

"About the wedding fever." Bea's shoulders were shaking with laughter. "I can't believe you told him. Sorry. I shouldn't laugh. But I can't help it." She tried to suppress a laugh, but instead a little snort came out.

"I don't have wedding fever! Why would I tell Aseem I have wedding fever when I don't?"

"Sorry, I shouldn't have said, 'told him.' What I meant was, I can't believe you let him know about your wedding fever." Then she let out one of her eardrum-piercing cackles and slapped her bony knee.

"That's it," Angela said, taking the key out of the ignition. "Either you stop saying 'wedding fever' or we're not going to Sacramento. That means no sunny road trip, no toying with any unsuspecting poker players at Thunder Valley, and *none of your favorite pizza!*"

"Good gravy, girlie. You went straight to eleven that time. OK, OK, I promise. No more comments about your... you know... *condition.*" Bea sounded solemn and put her head down. It wasn't more than a beat before she started guffawing again.

Angela scowled but started the car anyway and headed onto the road toward the freeway. "How about we change the subject? I had an interesting conversation with Lexie yesterday."

"Lemme guess. She thinks someone deliberately poisoned food at the mixer. And she thinks the inspector's a fake. And you're not mad at her anymore."

Angela's jaw dropped. "I'm not sure if I'm mad at her or not. But how'd you guess right about everything else?"

"Partly because I figured she'd be able to spot Inspector Pinocchio was a fake. Get it? Inspector Pinocchio?"

"Yes, Bea. I managed to decipher another of

your highbrow witticisms. A miracle has occurred."

"I'm liking this sarcastic side of yours—could it be the effects of wedding fever, oops, I mean—"

"It's not too late to turn around."

"Sorry, Angie. I'll try harder," Bea said, with a smirk that made clear she was hardly trying at all. "I'm sure you agree that Lexie's got an eye for scams. But the main reason I know what Lexie had to say is because I watched you two talking. Then I watched you walk away without asking her to leave again."

"You got all that from watching us?"

"Yep. One hundred percent," Bea said, tucking her chin to her chest and looking out the window. Despite her efforts to contain them, a few guffaws eventually leaked out.

"What's so funny?"

"I can't lie to you, Angie. The reason watching you helped was that I decided to talk to Lexie once I was sure you were gone." Bea gave her knee another slap.

"Oh, brother."

"I had a theory, Lexie had a theory, and we compared notes. We both knew right away that inspector was a phony. Scam like that happened at my favorite cardroom back in the day. Jerk from a rival place tried to get it shut down by contaminating the rice. Since the menu was mostly Asian cuisine, they got half the players in one Friday night session sick as dogs. But they were foiled by their pretend inspector. Anyone could tell he was fake as a three-dollar bill from a mile away."

"Lexie says the timing's off, too—that it probably isn't food poisoning, since everyone got sick so fast."

The sun hitting the car as they drove east was strong. Angela reached for one of the knobs on the dashboard. "Mind if I turn on the air?"

Bea hit the button to roll up her window. "Good idea. All this wind from the freeway might mess up my 'do."

Angela glanced at Bea with a raised eyebrow and a grin. Bea's helmet of gray hair, cut in the shape of a bowl, showed little sign of moving.

"I like Lexie's thinking about the food poisoning," Bea continued. "More evidence we're looking at a scam. Lexie and I had a good laugh over ol' Eric's 'buy my overpriced thermometer' hustle, too. Not what you'd expect from a real inspector. But there's one thing she couldn't have picked up on."

"What's that?"

"Dear old Rhonda. Don't you think it's kind of

convenient that she ditched the mixer before all the drama—you know, when everyone started tossing their—"

"Don't say it."

"Cookies. Just cookies, Angela. Why can't I say that word? Everyone loves cookies! Tossing 'em, not so much."

Bea couldn't contain her amusement with herself. "It means barfing. 'Tossing your cookies,' I mean."

Angela rolled her eyes. "I thought of Rhonda, too. What if she got sick herself? That might explain why she rushed off."

"I guess we'll find out at the wedding. She's still on top of my suspect list."

"What's her motive? Like you said, won't this just blow back on her and the other vendors?"

"Trust me, I can think of a bunch of possibilities. That's the fun part: the mystery we have to solve! And bringing Rhonda to justice, of course. That'll be the real hoot."

"So that's why you're suddenly so excited about observing wedding planning in action."

"I want to defend our reputation, Angie. And get some of my favorite pizza. Look, here's our exit!"

"I'm hungry, too. We'll have to hurry, though. I

want to get there before the wedding starts for a behind-the-scenes tour with Georgina. That leaves only about ninety minutes. I thought you'd want to stop for pizza on the way home instead."

"You're half right. I want to stop for pizza on the way home *also*."

They got to the little pizzeria moments after it opened and had the place to themselves. Over two huge, fragrant slices of New York-style pie, Angela presented her checklist for their wedding education field trip. She was reading notes off her phone and making edits, and in between taps, she carefully sopped the grease off the top of her slice with a white paper napkin.

"I'm really curious about how they choreograph everything and keep the guests moving in the right direction. I'm glad Georgina will be Rhonda's back-up today. She said that means she'll have time to show us the ropes."

"Mwrebaph," Bea said, after shoving her folded pepperoni slice into her mouth. She'd never embraced the custom of mopping the oil off a classic New York slice. As she guided the pizza back to the plate, a gooey strand of cheese with a shiny disk of pepperoni attached slid along a river of spicy orange grease. It slipped off the end of the slice and landed on the front of Bea's baggy t-shirt

—a pink one she'd selected in honor of the romantic occasion.

Angela sighed. "I don't suppose you brought another shirt."

"No such luck," Bea replied, her mouth still full of pizza. A few wet blobs threatened to escape from the side of her mouth. "Don't worry, Angie. I think it looks kind of nice," Bea added, looking down at the oily orange blotch. "It marks the spot where my boob once stood. Just two vacant lots there now. They've both moved downtown. Maybe I should drop a pepperoni slice on the other side—"

"Not necessary," Angela said. Her frown gave way to a chuckle. "It's not like we're guests at the wedding, anyway. We're supposed to be as inconspicuous as we can be. Like we're watching a play from the wings." She picked up the paper plate with the remains of her crust and started to stand up. "Ready?" Bea handed her plate over and they headed for the door.

"Aah," Bea said, taking a long sip from her soda. "This place is almost perfect. Too bad they don't have iced coffee."

They hopped back into the car and headed onto the freeway. "Tahoe traffic's starting to pick up," Angela said. "Glad we didn't dawdle over lunch. We still haven't talked about what you noticed in the walk-in. I saw you trying to hide something from Eric Delvecchio."

"You noticed that, huh? I think you're getting the detecting bug, too, Angie. The main thing I noticed was something in the mixing bowl—"

"Blood, right?"

"If you knew, why'd you ask me, girlie?" Bea laughed. "I was pretty sure by then that our friend Eric was not a real inspector. But just in case… I thought it would be better if he didn't see that."

"That's why you didn't want Aseem to eat the mousse, right?"

"That was one reason. I also figured maybe the desserts were poisoned. We don't know for sure how people got it, right? Did you see the little streak of leftover whipped cream in the bowl? Nice clean-up job those wedding people did."

"Thank you for looking out for him. Now that we're talking about it, I realize I should have thrown those mousses out, for safety's sake. I don't think any desserts were served, though— maybe that rules them out as a source of poison. At least I gave the mixer bowl a good scrub."

"Are you sure we shouldn't have saved it? We don't know how the blood got there."

"I just assumed someone got cut. I wanted to

make sure no one used the bowl without noticing it."

"Maybe it was our poisoner. For all we know, preparing poison is dangerous business," Bea said.

"Oh no! What if I destroyed evidence?"

"Don't worry, girlie. Nothing we can do about it now."

"I think I managed to learn something about our poisoner, though. Maybe I even figured out which food was poisoned."

"I'm listening."

"Someone tried to dispose of a bag that had some leaves in it. I checked with Perfection Produce—the salad vendors we recommended to the caterers—and sent them some pictures. It wasn't one of their bags, and they didn't recognize the greens."

"Poisonous salad? I love it! As if I needed another reason never to eat that rabbit food," Bea cackled.

"Of course, we can't be sure it was the salad—at least not yet. You know how chefs are here in California. Could just be some organic, heirloom-something-or-other that Perfection Produce hasn't tried yet. But I brought the bag with me, because I thought of someone who might know:

Fiona Wheaton. A florist knows all about plants, right?"

"Good thinking, Angie. Will Feefee the Flower Lady be at the wedding?"

"No, but I thought we could cruise out to Play-fair Pines afterwards. My mom was too busy with showings to see us, so I figured we'd have time. Fiona's expecting us. Don't worry—I haven't forgotten about poker. We'll cut back over to I-80 after visiting Fiona and land not far from Thunder Valley. It'll be a beautiful afternoon up at Fiona's farm, too."

With time to spare, Angela found a shaded spot on L street, not far from the capitol. Enjoying the view of the majestic dome and the pretty lawns around it, Bea deemed their parking ex-ceedingly lucky. "Runnin' good today. Glad I'll put my luck to use at poker later," she chuckled. From their parking spot the wedding site was just a few minutes' walk. "Glad I wore my best shoes." Bea picked up a foot to show Angela the cushiony treads of her velcro-fastened beige sneakers.

As they approached the garden, Angela noticed a white pavilion, gleaming in the midday sun. "How pretty! That must be where they do the cer-emony." People were milling around the edges of the garden, some of them dressed for a wedding, others looking like curious passersby. Workers were setting up wooden folding chairs along a walkway set apart by stanchions and white and gold velvet ropes. "That must be where the bride walks down the aisle."

"Feeling feverish—" Bea started to say.

Angela scowled at Bea and clucked her tongue. "Look, there's Georgina."

Georgina was buzzing around the venue, phone and notebook in gloved hands, a headset wrapped around her head.

Angela leaned down to whisper to Bea, "Is it just me, or does she look stressed?" She caught her old friend's eye and waved, and she and Bea rushed over to greet her.

"You were right, Georgina. This is a lovely spot for a ceremony."

"I'd hardly know," she blurted. "It's not like I can't handle a wedding by myself. I just… I had no idea Rhonda's notes would be so… useless. I don't know half of what the bride expects. And this is only the beginning—the reception will be an even bigger challenge."

"Rhonda will be here soon, though, right?"

"No," Georgina said. "I mean—I don't think so. I've tried texting her, but she's not answering. I don't know where she is."

"I'm sorry, Georgina. I'd like to offer my help, but I'm not sure what good it would be. I didn't bring my white gloves, after all," Angela said, looking at Georgina's hands. "Impressive. At least everyone will know you're giving top-shelf service."

Georgina reflexively scratched her gloved hands. "Oh—ha—these things? I... I just got a bit of a rash. Poison ivy mixed in with all these roses or something. Calamine lotion—it's not a pretty look. The gloves cover it up and keep me from scratching."

"No one would know. Looks classy. Like that old movie star Audrey Hepburn."

"Or Minnie Mouse," cracked Bea.

"Funny," Georgina said sourly. "There's the officiant. You're both welcome to observe what you like, as long as you stay out of the way. That goes for the reception, too—it's at the Gold Rush Ballroom, right around the corner. I'm too busy to escort you." Georgina hustled over to meet the robe-clad officiant at the edge of the garden.

Bea and Angela moved to the edge of the walkway behind the pavilion, trying to maintain their low profile. They watched Georgina pointing energetically as she gave instructions to the officiant. The officiant nodded, her expression tensing. Georgina started to walk away, and the officiant put her hand on her arm—a gentle gesture that Georgina seemed to dismiss as she hustled off.

"Somebody's in a mood," Bea chortled under her breath. "Is she mad because Rhonda didn't show up, or just annoyed that Rhonda left bad notes?"

Angela shrugged. "Georgina doesn't seem too worried about Rhonda. But maybe she's too stressed about handling the entire wedding to think about anything else. I hope Rhonda's not sick, though."

"Me, too. It would blow my theory that she's the culprit."

A few minutes later, Georgina surprised them from behind. She was carrying two large baskets full of small white-and-pink boxes.

"Angela, if you're still willing to help, here's a way you can. Could you put one on each chair?" She held the two baskets out to Angela.

"Of course." Angela handed one of the baskets to Bea and picked one of the boxes out of hers. "Disposable digital cameras. I've never heard of these. Don't they have a professional photographer? I thought that was him over there."

Angela tilted her head in the direction of a

good-looking young man with a camera around his neck. He had walked in with two of the bridesmaids and was chatting them up, looking completely relaxed.

"Yeah. Ben Billings. He's—he's not exactly new, but this is one of his first weddings on his own. He was Sandy Givens' assistant for a few weddings. Hardly any on-the-job experience, but he was thirsty to get out on his own. Rhonda decided to help him. Rhonda and I have been carting these disposables to every wedding for a few years now. Honestly, I thought we'd never need them, but I'm glad to have them today. Hopefully, Ben will catch all the big moments, but this way, maybe somebody will catch any he misses."

Georgina went back to coordinating the rest of the preparation while Angela and Bea put a camera on each of the eighty-odd white chairs.

"I bet that's what Sandy was going to tell me yesterday," Bea said. "Rhonda lured her assistant away. That lady has a real weakness for the virile young dudes. Dang. Too bad Sandy's not here to give us the backstory."

"And too bad Rhonda's not here. I don't think we'll learn much standing on the sidelines. I was hoping for a bit more wedding-planning education."

"Yeah, I agree. Too bad Rhonda's not here. I was hoping for a bit more poison-planning education."

"We don't know that she's the poisoner," Angela hissed. "Won't you feel bad if it turns out she's been sick from it herself?"

"Come to think of it, I think it's clearer now that Rhonda's our evil-doer. Why wouldn't she just tell Georgina if she was sick? Even if she was in the hospital, she could have answered a text."

"Ha! Says the woman who refuses to even use a cell phone!"

"Angela? It's Connie. I'll be quick because I'm rushing to my connection."

Angela held her phone up so she and Bea could listen to Connie's message on the speaker as they walked back to the car. "My contractor called. He stopped at my place to pick up some tools and noticed one of your guests' cars was still there. And it's weird, but he said it's parked in the garage of my new house—my shell of a new house, I mean. The car's covered with a tarp, possibly something the crew left on the site. But the car must belong to one of the mixer guests—he already asked his whole crew, and none of them left theirs there.

"I don't mean to be a pest, but he says it has to be moved because they're starting work on that part of the house first thing Monday. Do you mind if I ask your front desk manager to tell the guest to move it? Text me and let me know, OK? Oh—gotta run, they're calling my flight. I can't wait to be back in California. I'm sending you a big hug, and looking forward to seeing you soon!"

"That's strange," Angela said to Bea. "I thought all the wedding vendors had left by the end of the day yesterday. Today's Saturday, after all. I thought they all had weddings to work today."

They reached the car and Angela unlocked it with a chirp. They settled into their seats, and Angela quickly tapped out a text reply.

```
Hi Connie! Pls feel free to ask
    Jackson to help you. He can
   figure out if the car belongs
  to a guest and ask them to move
        it if so. See you soon.
```

"Should I have told her that it probably wasn't one of our guests' cars?"

"Nah. She'll be back at the inn in a few hours,

right?" said Bea. "I'm sure you'll hear from her again if there's anything you can do to help."

They found the wedding reception hall around a corner just a few blocks from where they started. "Oh my, we're here already. We could have left the car where it was, I suppose. But look —another great parking space."

"Lucky omen number two!" Bea said. "Let's take a peek at this reception, then skedaddle to Feefee's flower bed, Angie. I've got a feeling I'm gonna clean up at poker tonight."

CHAPTER 10

"I don't know why everyone I know in San Francisco says it's boring up here in Gold Country," Angela said. "There are so many historical things to see, and not just the state capital. This road, for example. It's part of the Pony Express Trail."

"Fascinating. I thought we were driving on a dull, two-lane road in the middle of West Nowhere, when, in fact, it's a path once used by *mailmen*," Bea said with mock awe. "I can die happy now, Angie. My life is complete."

"Did you know you can follow the route of the Pony Express all the way to Missouri? You don't have to be so cynical, you know. You're not too old to learn something."

"And just because your hair is in a bun, you don't have to act like a school marm."

"Maybe you're just jealous. Sacramento's a lot more exciting than Fresno."

"Weren't you just complaining about people from the Bay Area saying Sacramento's boring? Isn't that a little hypocritical to be dissing my hometown?"

"You're right. I'm sorry."

"Just kidding, girlie. I hear Fresberg's more exciting now. When I left, there was nothing there but raisins." Bea flipped down the visor, examined her face in the mirror, and let loose a bark of laughter. "Few more wrinkles and I could pass as a golden raisin myself."

Angela followed the navigation system's instructions and turned onto a smaller local road. "We're on the edge of Playfair Pines now. Hard to believe we're less than an hour from Sacramento. We're really out in the country."

Tall evergreens and huge plots of gently rolling acreage lined both sides of the road, with scarcely a building for several miles. Finally, they spotted a large, pretty farmhouse. Next to it bloomed a field of lavender so vivid, it looked like a purple carpet from a distance. As they approached the house,

Angela noticed six or seven cars parked close together along the far side.

"I didn't realize Fiona would have other visitors. When she said just to pop over when we left the reception, I thought that meant she'd be alone."

Angela slid her small SUV into the open slot at the end of the row. She and Bea hopped out and walked toward the house's dramatic wraparound porch. As they reached the stairs, the door sprang open. A small crowd of laughing people—several women of various ages, and a young, affectionate couple who looked to be a bride and groom—streamed out of the farmhouse. Fiona stood behind them, holding the door.

"Thank you, Fiona," said the bride, smiling joyously and leaning against her fiancé's shoulder. "I know it's going to be just beautiful. I can't believe ours will be the first wedding held here."

"It's my honor," Fiona replied, smiling in her gracious, serene way. Her hair was pulled back into a thick, messy braid. Standing in the doorway, she looked almost like a picture, framed by the doorway and the roses climbing the trellises on each side of it. "I'll keep you posted on the construction. As soon as the conservatory is upright, I'll invite you back up to start planning."

Angela absently mouthed "conserva-tree," unconsciously imitating Fiona's melodious way of speaking. Bea noticed and chuckled. Angela snapped out of her daze, frowning and giving Bea a gentle nudge with her elbow.

As the group descended toward their cars, the bride called back to Fiona, "I can't wait to see it, Fiona. The drawings were just lovely. They remind me of the Conservatory of Flowers, one of my favorite buildings in San Francisco—it will be the perfect setting for our wedding."

"Sounds amazing," Angela whispered to Bea.

"I'm inspired by weddings I attended in Kew Gardens, back in England," Fiona said. "Have you been?"

Bea looked expectantly at Angela, who, sure enough, was mouthing "bean." Angela winced and shook her head at being spotted again. Bea failed to suppress a snort.

"Of course, here we'll have all this grand outdoor beauty as well," Fiona continued. "You'll be able to see the pines through the glass dome of the conservatory. It does sound lovely, doesn't it?"

The bridal group drove off and Fiona welcomed Angela and Bea to come into the farmhouse. "Thank you for your patience."

"Not at all. I didn't realize you were already

booking weddings here. You work fast," Angela said, smiling.

"I'm sure I could learn a trick or two from you. I hear you got the inn open in record time." Angela basked in Fiona's compliment. "My farm won't actually open for weddings for many months. That bride works for my husband's tech company. She may look like your average blushing bride," Fiona said confidentially, "but she's got the brain of a finance genius in that pretty head of hers. Ex-Wall Street. My husband says she's improved his numbers dramatically since she's been leading his finance team. When she said she wanted to be the first to get married at my flower farm, I could hardly refuse. Those quarterly earnings reports mean everything to a public company CEO."

"Your husband's CEO of a public company? I guess you're not the only big success in the family," Angela said.

Fiona cocked her head and crinkled her nose. "Yes, I suppose there's no denying my husband's business is a success."

They walked into the large, airy space, past several mostly-empty tall floral chillers, an over-sized island with a granite countertop and two sinks, and two large built-in shelving units that held various containers for flower arrangements. Fiona motioned for them to sit at the imposing, rustic table in the center of the room. One end of it was covered with flowers that Fiona had apparently been arranging. There was also a tablet on a little stand, looking tiny in the center of the massive table.

Angela ignored Fiona's invitation and walked past the table to the tall wall of windows in the back of the room. They revealed a huge open field extending to the perimeter of acres of evergreen woods, far in the distance. On the left side was the huge swath of lavender that Angela and Bea had seen from the car.

"Oh, my goodness," Angela said. "I see what you meant about outdoor beauty."

"Not too shabby," Bea chimed in. She pointed at what looked like a construction site at the far end of the enormous lawn. "Is that where you shall locate the conserva-tree?" She was making her best attempt at a British accent. It wasn't good. Angela shook her head and looked at Bea with a forbearing grin, then sheepishly at Fiona, hoping her feelings weren't hurt.

"Aw, it ain't the worst accent oy evah 'eard,"

Fiona said, leaning forward with her hands on her hips, her legs slightly splayed and her elbows wide. "Try it wif me, Bea. *The rine in spine sties minely in the pline.*"

The three of them laughed until they were nearly crying. Eventually Fiona sighed and said, "Why thank you, Bea. I love an excuse to trot out my Eliza Doolittle imitation." Her cheeks were rosy from laughing, and her charming intonation had returned. "Angela, shall we take a look at that plant of yours?" The three of them pulled up their chairs and Angela handed Fiona the bag.

"Oh yes, I recognize this. Not something we see in England, and I don't believe it's native to California, either. I heard of it recently—at a wedding mixer, of all places." She held the bag up toward the sunlight for closer inspection. "If it's the plant I'm thinking of, it's called needleweed. Some people call it freegan salad."

"Salad? So you're saying it's edible?" said Bea.

"In a way," Fiona said. "The young leaves are, but needleweed must be cooked very carefully, otherwise it's poisonous. Good job you kept it in that bag, Angela. They say you shouldn't even let it touch your skin before it's cooked. Especially if your skin is broken—which can happen, because the stalks have tiny thorns." She held the bag up in front of Angela. "See? These leaves have been carefully trimmed, but you can see a little stalk attached to that one—see the little thorn?"

"And if you eat it without cooking it?" Angela said.

"Most likely, you'll feel quite vommy—" Fiona said.

"She means you'll hurl!" Bea said, earning a resigned chuckle from Angela.

"Indeed. Most likely, it will make you quite sick. But if I remember properly, it can even be lethal in some cases," Fiona said. "Older people, people with certain illnesses, and such. It's much more dangerous for them."

Angela gulped, her eyes wide. "You mentioned you heard about it at a mixer," she said after a pause. "How so?"

"Right, it was last fall. We were at one of the less popular wedding sites, a casual sort of place. Just an old house with a large backyard, really. There are a few such places around Sacramento, usually owned by older people who want to host low-budget weddings and bring in a little income. Rhonda has disdain for them, of course, but occasionally deigns to let one of them host a mixer—especially if she thinks few people plan to attend.

"I remember the needleweed. It was growing

on the edge of the yard. It grows quickly. Once it starts, before you know it, you can have a hedge. And it has the loveliest purple berries at its peak. They're quite poisonous, too, and the bushes at this place were full of them. The host knew people might be curious, so she warned us all not to touch them. Rhonda was especially interested, as I recall."

"See, Angie? Another sign that Rhonda is our poisoner. That's why she didn't show up at the wedding today."

"But Bea, we can't rule her out as a poison *victim*."

"I wouldn't want to guess either way," Fiona said evenly. "There are people like to eat poisonous plants like needleweed—plants that are dangerous, but can be made harmless if prepared properly. It's an adrenaline rush, I suppose."

"Sort of like people who eat blowfish. One bite of badly prepared sushi can kill you—and you pay hundreds of dollars just to try it," Angela said.

"Exactly. I think freegan salad is kind of the vegetarian version of that."

"Like our Rhonda's a vegetarian," scoffed Bea. "We already know she's a wannabe maneater. My money's on scare tactics. Or maybe she wanted to sabotage you, Angie—just in case you got any ideas about doing weddings without her."

"Sounds very sinister for our little wedding world," Fiona said. "There's no denying Rhonda's a tough customer, though. Still, there are people who believe needleweed is a miracle plant that can cure all kinds of diseases—AIDS, cancer, acne—"

"That's it!" cackled Bea. "The blockhead wanted a cure for blackheads!"

The tablet on the tabletop beeped softly and lit up. Fiona tapped it and Sandy's face appeared on the screen. She looked pale and a bit tired, but otherwise none the worse for wear.

"Hullo, Sandy," Fiona said. "Are you feeling better?"

"Much," Sandy said. "I'm calling because I've got some pictures of your barn wedding set-up ready for you."

"Hi, Sandy!" Angela said, leaning over Fiona's shoulder. "Good to see you're home from the hospital."

Fiona pulled her phone from her pocket. "It's my husband texting. Why don't you three chat while I answer him?" She turned the tablet to face Angela and Bea and stepped away from the table.

"How nice to see you both. I had no idea you'd be up in our part of the world."

"Bea and I are so glad you're out of the hospital. We were getting worried—"

"Angie just heard that the poison that made you blow chunks could have killed you!"

"Classy, Bea," Angela snickered, shaking her head.

"Bea, don't ever censor yourself on my account," Sandy smiled. "But poison—don't you mean the bad food?"

"Looks like it was bad salad," Bea said. "As in salad that shouldn't have been salad."

"Bea, are you saying the salad was contaminated? Or—you're not saying someone did something to it—"

"On purpose?" Bea said. "Yeah, that's what we're saying. I've got a good idea who, and we're trying to figure out why."

"Technically, we don't know who or why yet, Bea," Angela said. "Sandy, we think it was a poisonous plant called needleweed. We found some leaves in our kitchen."

Sandy's eyes were wide. "That's just…. Wow. Needleweed. I need to call Dennis to make sure he's OK. Hey, I've got an idea. Why don't you stop here on your way back to Napa? Then you could sign my books for me. I'm in Folsom, down the hill a bit. It's on your way. What do you say?"

"I'm sorry, Sandy, but we're heading to Thunder Valley next. Bea needs a fix of poker. It's been months since she's snuck up on any unsuspecting grinders," Angela said.

"Don't worry about me, girlie," Bea said. "I can play poker any time. Don't you think we should check on Sandy in person?"

"Sure," Angela said, looking confused. "By the way, Sandy, we came up to observe a wedding with Rhonda and Georgina. But Rhonda never showed up. To be honest, I'm a bit worried she might have gotten ill, too."

"Angie, if Rhonda's sick, she probably just overdosed on all that eye candy she can't resist. Speaking of which, Sandy, we got to see your former apprentice in action. Good-looking, but Georgina seemed to think he lacks training. I know there's a story there—so if you want those autographs, you're gonna have to spill your guts. And I don't mean regurgitate!"

"It's a deal," Sandy laughed. "Angela, if you're really worried about Rhonda, you can stop by her place on your way home. It's not far from here." Fiona returned to the table and the four of them said their goodbyes, with Sandy promising to email the pictures later.

"Ask Sandy if you can have copies, too, Angela," Fiona said. "Knowing Sandy's work, I'm sure they'd make lovely promotional images for the inn —at least, if you decide to do weddings."

"Thank you for everything, Fiona. Bea and I should say goodbye now—or should we say, *cheers?*" Angela said.

"Must you rush off? I thought you'd want to wait for Aseem to return," Fiona said. "He went with my husband into town for coffee. I just asked him to bring us a snack for tea."

"He couldn't be with Aseem," Angela said. "Aseem's in Silicon Valley today, hanging out with tech dudes."

"Gary is a tech dude through and through," Fiona said with a lilting laugh. "And normally he's on the Peninsula on Saturdays. Turns out he has a meeting on Monday at one of his facilities in Sacramento, so he decided to stay up here with me."

Angela's eyes grew wide. "Wait—your husband is *Gary* Wheaton? As in *the* Gary Wheaton?"

"He's just *my* Gary Wheaton to me," Fiona smiled. "Since you've figured out his secret, it won't surprise you that he homed in on your brilliant boyfriend at the mixer. Gary's always on the lookout for new talent. He says if you find a great person, hire them—even if you don't have the perfect job opening."

"Hire them?" Angela said with a slight frog in her voice. She coughed quietly to try to disguise it.

"I think you were right—we should get going, Angie," Bea said, grabbing her elbow and nudging her toward the door. "We don't want to get back too late, right?"

Angela barely nodded.

"Fiona, tell Aseem we said hello, and we'll see him back at the ranch!"

"Achoo!!"

Gary Wheaton pulled a handkerchief from his pocket and blew his nose. "Thanks for meeting up here. Turns out I need to be at one of our local facilities on Monday. I love being with Fee on her turf, but all the trees and plants up here—I think I'm allergic to every one of them. No denying my nerd DNA. I wasn't designed to spend much time outdoors—or marry a florist," he added with a laugh.

"It was no trouble at all," Aseem said.

The drive from Napa to the Sierra foothills

was only about half an hour longer than to Gary's office in Silicon Valley, not that it mattered to Aseem. He would have driven all morning and all night to meet Gary Wheaton for coffee. In fact, in that moment he was considering pinching himself to confirm he was awake.

He could hardly believe the stories he was hearing—true-life tales of 24x7 coding sessions in a Palo Alto garage, back when the programmers he'd grown up idolizing were barely out of college, and Silicon Valley was still a lot like the Wild West.

And he was hearing them straight from Gary Wheaton—the real Gary Wheaton, in the flesh!

Gary took a sip from the paper coffee cup in front of him and frowned. "Green tea. Yuck. Why can't bio-hacking involve espresso?" Gary laughed. "Enough about me. Tell me about you. I want to hear about your app ideas. But start with the personal stuff—how'd you and Angela meet?"

Most amazing of all, Gary Wheaton was asking about him.

"We were both scrappy contractors," Aseem began. "Angel was doing marketing for small businesses. I was setting up office networks, websites, all that tech stuff small companies need. We were both constantly hustling for projects."

Aseem explained how he'd noticed right away how smart and hardworking Angela was, and how much her clients valued her help. They trusted each other with their clients, with Angela planning out their websites and Aseem building them. Over time, through late nights and tight deadlines, their friendship grew—eventually becoming something more. "She knew before I did," Aseem said.

"Women always do. It's been more than two decades, but I can still remember how exciting it was to work with Fee in the early days," Gary said. "I wanted it to last forever."

"Angel and I talked about how we wanted to be part of something bigger, of building a lasting business. It was something we shared, you know? Then Betty Snickerdoodle came along, and Angela saw the potential right away. She saw how loyal the readers were and knew the audience could be huge. She's just... she's just so brilliant at marketing, at building things—"

"Not that you're biased."

"I'm biased," Aseem smiled. "I just believe in her so much. More than she believes in herself, I think."

"Dude, you sound like a man in love," Gary

laughed. "Happens to the best of us. Fee and I fell in love on the job, too."

"It's not like we've said it to each other or anything. We're still at the beginning. But I know... I know I don't want to lose her."

"Why would you?"

"I want to help her with the business. She's so brilliant—she's the only one who doesn't seem to realize it—and I love being part of her vision. But sometimes it's like, I dunno—"

"A minefield?"

Aseem shrugged. "Sounds crazy, but yes. Plus —I didn't expect this, but helping her bring her vision to life seems to have inspired all these new ideas of my own. That's what got me tinkering with these apps on the side."

"I told you, I've been there, just in Angela's shoes. Fiona was my most valuable employee in the early days. But if she hadn't had the chance to chase her own ambitions, we might not even be together now."

"The thing is, I saw it from the start. Like you said, it's hard to have a relationship with the boss."

"Fee could tell you that better than I could. I was holding on tight at first—afraid we'd break up if I let her go. Now I see that loosening up was what saved our relationship. Simple as that, really," Gary said. "Look, why don't you tell me about your app ideas—that's why you're here, right?"

"I'm so sorry—TMI, right?"

"No, no, that's not it. Don't forget—I asked," Gary said, laughing. "If there's any advice I'd give young people these days, it's to make time for your relationships. Don't get me wrong, I've got no regrets about pursuing my ambitions. I don't pretend I haven't been richly rewarded for it, either. But what's money good for if not solving problems? If I like your ideas, we can help each other. So let's hear 'em!"

Aseem explained his app concepts, carefully emphasizing the business needs they would serve. He'd rehearsed in his head the entire drive up—and now his presentation was going perfectly. Gary listened and nodded, sometimes asking for details. The more they talked, the more confident in his ideas Aseem sounded—and the more excited, too.

"I know a good prospect when I see one, Aseem, and I'm not one for over-analyzing. I go with my gut, and my gut says you're someone I want to work with."

"That's great—so I assume this means you want to invest?" Aseem felt his adrenaline begin to rise. He had to work to keep his knees from knocking under the table. "What's my next step? Do I write up a business plan?"

"I say we think bigger. I've been wanting to start an incubator to develop lots of apps, from lots of company founders. Yours could be the first ones, of course, but I need someone who's been in the trenches to run the incubator—and I think it should be you."

"Full-time? Run an incubator?" Aseem said, after a pause. Gary nodded. "I—I thought we were talking about an investment."

"Pivot is my middle name, Aseem. I don't have to tell you, we've gotta move fast in tech. This is going to be great—like I like to say, 'crazy great.' I've got an office space in San Francisco that's ready to build out. Of course, if you wanted to move it across the Golden Gate Bridge to be closer to Napa, I could be persuaded. Boy, do I feel fantastic! No worse for skipping that wheat grass —no better medicine for the gray matter than an exciting new business."

Gary stood up from the café table, looking ready for action. "Just give me a minute to pick up the snacks Fee asked for. Then we'll head back to the farm and tell Angela your good news in person."

"Sure," Aseem said. "Wait—*what?* In person?"

His eyes widened, and he felt a droplet of sweat forming on his brow.

"Didn't I tell you? Fee invited Angela and Bea to stop by the farm. They're expecting us any minute."

CHAPTER 11

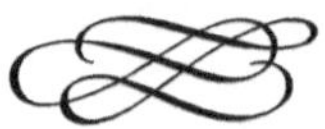

"Thank you for making our excuses to Fiona. But please know, I don't want to talk about it," Angela said glumly. She walked ahead of Bea down the steps from the farmhouse toward her car. "Let's just go to Sandy's, get your book-signing done, and head home."

"Angie, let's not rush off yet. I just wanted to get you outside to talk for a minute. You know I'm not one for sugar-coating. But sugar-coating's not needed in this case—"

"Oh, look," Angela said, spotting Aseem's car at the end of the now-empty parking area. "If only we'd gotten here after that bridal party left, I would have seen his car and avoided Fiona's humiliating revelation. No sugar-coating is needed is right, Bea. I'm a big girl. I can handle the truth."

"That's not what I mean. No sugar-coating is needed because Aseem must have a good explanation—and look," Bea added, pointing to a six-figure SUV heading toward the driveway, "he's here now to give it to you."

"Come down now, Bea, please. Let's go!"

But whether because she wanted to give Aseem a chance to explain or simply because she didn't like being bossed around by anyone, not even Angela, Bea made no effort to rush down the porch steps. If anything, she seemed to move slower. By the time she took the last step onto the path, Aseem and Gary were shutting the doors of Gary's car, and Fiona had stepped out of the farmhouse onto the porch.

"Angel," Aseem said, his face tense. "I'm sorry. Let me explain."

"I can't imagine how. It's bad enough that you lied about where you were going. Fiona says Gary wants to hire you—is that right? You're looking for *a job*?"

"I wasn't—it wasn't like that. I wasn't looking for a job, and I wasn't trying to hide anything from you. I just—I didn't want to get ahead of myself. I was just going to share my app ideas with Gary. You know, the ones I've been noodling—my side hustle. I figured it probably wouldn't amount to anything, and we'd just have a laugh later over my brush with greatness."

"You're not giving yourself enough credit," Gary interjected. "You told me Angela doesn't have as much confidence as she should. I'd say you both could work on that."

Angela's jaw dropped and she stared at Aseem. "Nice to know you've been discussing me with a virtual stranger."

"Gary, darling," Fiona called out in her melodious way, "why don't you bring those snacks in here? I can use some help, and maybe Aseem and Angela could use a moment alone."

"In a few minutes, honey," Gary said, missing his wife's gentle hint. "Aseem said nothing but the nicest things, Angela. But better than that, I think we've come up with a perfect solution to your relationship issues."

Mouth still agape, Angela let out a noisy gasp.

"Relationship issues?" Angela cried, staring at Aseem. "And here I was thinking you were just unhappy with your job!"

"Uh-oh," Gary said. "Did Awkward Gary just strike again? I'm sorry, Aseem."

Angela hurried to the driver's side of her car and hopped in—just in time to avoid Aseem seeing her tears start to fall. Bea climbed in the passenger side. They turned their backs to the windows. Angela ignored Aseem's knocking on hers.

"Don't cry, girlie." Bea patted Angela's knee in as soothing a gesture as she could muster. "I know you and Aseem will work things out. You haven't heard his side of the story yet."

Angela's quiet crying turned to sobs. Aseem peered anxiously through the car window and knocked on it again. "What can he possibly say? I thought we were a team. I thought we were the best team. All the while, he was thinking about getting a new job. And even worse, he told Gary we have relationship problems!"

"Don't forget, Angie, we don't know what Aseem actually told Gary. We only heard it from Gary, and he's obviously a doofus."

Angela's crying slowed and she chuckled a little. "Bea, you're talking about one of the tech industry's most famous geniuses."

"Yes, the good news is I hear that he's building all the robots. If Gary's programming them, they're not going to defeat us humans any time soon."

Angela laughed again and blew her nose. "I don't know what I'm going to do," she added, her tone sad again.

"You don't have to decide anything now. We've got books to sign and a mystery to solve. And a wild beast named Rhonda to corral!"

"Good idea. Let's focus on that." Angela nodded and turned to face forward in her seat, then started the car. She knocked on the window and let Aseem know she was about to back up, then swung the visor toward the window to block his face. She could hear him pleading with her to wait, but she just shook her head and sighed as she backed the car out of the driveway.

"Bea, you're right about our mystery. We've still got to figure out who our poisoner is. I know you don't agree, but I think we should also make sure Rhonda's OK. We don't know for sure she's our culprit."

"Fine by me, girlie."

THEY WERE MOSTLY QUIET FOR THE NEXT HALF hour as they drove west down the grade.

Angela pointed to the dashboard. "We're getting more than 100 miles to the gallon," she said, as if trying to cheer herself up. "If I took my foot off the gas, I wonder if we would roll all the way to Sacramento."

"Back in the day, guys I played poker with would have bet money on that," Bea chuckled.

Angela's smartphone vibrated in its cradle. She touched it and Connie's face appeared. "Hi, y'all! How's your wedding field trip going?"

Angela didn't answer at first. "Hi, Connie," she finally sighed.

"Hey, that's not the kind of greeting I've come to expect from my new best friend."

"I'm sorry. Just a bit distracted. Any news about that mysterious car in your garage?"

"That's why I'm calling. Jackson said everyone left by yesterday evening, so it looks like the car doesn't belong to one of your mixer guests. Angela, he also said nearly half the attendees got a stomach bug—and several even went to the hospital! Is that right?"

"I was going to tell you later—"

"It was a regular barf-o-rama," Bea interjected.

"I'm afraid Bea's telling the truth. But don't worry—it's not contagious. We're thinking it was—"

"Poison!" blurted Bea.

"Whoa."

"I know. We discovered a poisonous plant that we think someone mixed into the salad. Now we just need to figure out who did it, and why. We're on our way to meet a photographer who was at the mixer, Sandy Givens—poor thing, she was one of the people who went to the hospital. She asked Bea to come sign her books, but while we're there—"

"We'll pump her for information about who and why. Except I am pretty sure it was Rhonda. Connie, you've met her. Not hard to picture her doing it, right?" Bea said.

"I don't know about poisoning, but Rhonda is an odd duck, bless her heart. Are you thinking she was trying to…to kill someone?"

"Fiona Wheaton told us the plant makes people very ill, but doesn't usually kill. The more I think about it, though, the more worried I feel. We don't know if all of the people who went to the hospital have recovered. And Bea, do you remember the EMTs saying one of the victims had a heart condition?"

"Rhonda might be a murderer!" Bea said with inappropriate glee.

Angela sighed. "Despite what Bea says, I think Rhonda deserves the benefit of the doubt. She was supposed to meet with us at the wedding today and didn't show. I'm afraid she might have been poisoned, too. We're going to stop at her house to check on her."

"Angela, do you think you should involve the police?" Connie said. "If you have evidence of poisoning, that sounds criminal."

"I called Sergeant McGregor yesterday and told him my suspicions. He said, 'Sabotage? Intentional poisoning? That's what every establishment with a food-borne illness scandal on their hands likes to think.' And he laughed at me. Honestly, I think he was enjoying it. That's why we're looking into the mystery ourselves. If we get enough evidence, he'll have to take it seriously. So Connie, what will you do about the car?"

"When I finish unpacking, I'll walk up to my place with the pups. I'll uncover the car and have a look. Who knows, I might get to solve a mystery of my own. If I can't figure out whose car it is, I'm not sure what I'll do, but at least I'll have a nice walk. There are still a few hours left of this beautiful wine country day. Oh, Angela, I'm happy to be back—to be home."

"I'm happy you're back, too, Connie. I'm sorry I didn't say so before."

"Angela, is everything OK?"

Angela sighed. "Been a rough day. The poisoning's not even the half of it. I'd love to have a good girl chat with you when we get home tonight."

"I'll pop the corn and pop a cork."

"Sounds good. And if you haven't figured out what to do about the car by then, I'll help. One more thing—avoid the inn kitchen for now, OK? Especially the walk-in cooler. We still don't know if other foods were tampered with."

As they continued down the freeway toward Sandy's place, Angela was quiet. Bea tried to coax her into a conversation.

"I told you, I don't want to talk about Aseem. Why are you taking his side? You're the one who's always telling me I'm too trusting."

"Maybe I should be glad you're seeing the light. Hey, I guess that means we don't even need to go to Rhonda's place. We've got more than enough reason to believe she's our poisoner. I say we rat her out to the police when we get home—maybe we should just call Sergeant McGregor right now—"

"She's not the most likeable person, Bea, but that hardly means she's the poisoner. Innocent until proven guilty, right? Everyone deserves the benefit of the doubt."

"Everyone?" Bea said sweetly.

"I see what you're doing," Angela scoffed. "Fine. I'll talk to him. But I'm still not going to talk about it with *you*."

"You win, girlie. Isn't that our turn?"

They headed down Sandy's quiet suburban street, passing a dozen older homes packed close together, to the cul-de-sac at the end. Sandy's two-story house was plain, but it had a large yard shaded by an enormous tree. A creek ran beside the house and under the road.

"Welcome!" Sandy said, holding open a door behind the garage. "Come in this way, through my studio."

The space was small and efficiently designed. A large closet had been converted into a narrow office with three workstations. Heavy drapes covered all the windows. A portrait studio, with a screen, a reflective umbrella and large lights, dominated the rear of the room.

"Nice set-up, Sandy. Might come in handy when we interrogate you about Rhonda," Bea said. "With that umbrella, we can make sure the light's right in your eyes."

Sandy laughed. "Let me just save my work. It will take a few minutes with these big photographs. My Betty Snickerdoodle books are on the coffee table."

Bea plopped into a plush chair in front of Sandy's towering stack of *Treacle Town* books, and Angela pulled a marker out of her purse. She always carried one whenever she went anywhere with Bea, just in case.

"Good gravy, Sandy," Bea chuckled, signing one of the books. "You might have paid for the down payment on the inn."

"Sandy, I'm happy to send any you're missing," Angela said.

"Just one or two of the early ones—I've got an automatic preorder for new ones. My husband says it's an addiction." A few minutes later, she pulled up a chair to join them. "At least we don't have to worry about being interrupted. My assistant doesn't work on Saturdays, and, well, I don't need to tell you I don't have an apprentice any longer."

"That's what I want to hear about," Bea said, putting the book in her hand in the "done" pile and grabbing another to sign.

"You're really gonna make me tell you? I mean, this industry seems all sweetness and light, and it mostly is. Most of us are in it to make happy memories for brides and grooms and be in love with love. But a few people can make it surprisingly rough-and-tumble—"

"Like, say, Rhonda?" Bea said.

"Why don't you tell us how you're feeling, first? We're sorry you had to go to the hospital," Angela said gently. Bea looked at Angela with a raised eyebrow, but kept quiet and grabbed another book.

"I'm fine now. Thank you for asking."

"We are pretty sure the poison was needle-weed, just in case you want to tell your doctor. We found leaves in the kitchen, and Fiona recognized it."

"I've been asking myself why that sounds familiar since you said it."

"Fiona said she heard about it at a wedding mixer last fall. She said the owner of the property warned everyone to stay away from it. Were you there, too?"

"Now that you mention it, I remember that mixer. The plants were growing like crazy around the edge of the property. They had these pretty purple berries. I don't think it was the owner who warned us, though. I believe it was Paige—the caterer. I remember her talking about those berries, about how they looked like they'd be delicious, but to stay away from them. Rhonda seemed fascinated by the plants, if I recall correctly."

Bea looked up and sent a smug look in Angela's direction.

"Do you suppose that means Rhonda could have been involved in the poisoning?" Angela replied. "Or, how about a different question? If we assume—just hypothetically—that Rhonda used the needleweed to poison food at the mixer, why would she do it? If the needleweed was mixed in with the baby salad greens, she couldn't target anyone in particular. Anyone who ate salad could be poisoned. Plus, what if whomever she wanted to poison didn't eat salad?"

"Only hypothetically, right?" said Sandy. "I'm not saying whether I think Rhonda could have done this."

"Sure sounds like you're afraid of her," Bea interrupted.

"Maybe I shouldn't say anything—"

"Just finish your thought, Sandy," Angela said. "We're just trying to figure out what happened. Rhonda won't hear anything you tell us. Right, Bea?"

"As sweet Betty Snickerdoodle, I solemnly swear," Bea said, putting her hand over her heart. "We won't say a peep."

Sandy began slowly. "You're right that she couldn't be certain who would get poisoned salad. But Rhonda knew who usually ate salad. We all see each other at these mixers every month. And there are some people, like the DJs, who often don't get food at all unless the caterers save them some leftovers. So she could safely assume they *wouldn't* be poisoned."

"Would she know you'd eat salad?"

"Everyone knows I try to eat healthier whenever I can. With two teenage boys and an overgrown teenager for a husband, there's not a lot of interest in salad in this house."

"Why would Rhonda want to poison you?" Bea said. "To make sure you don't complain that she lured your fetching former apprentice away?"

"I doubt it. I made sure not to let anyone know how upset I was about Ben, even though I'm pretty sure he stole my prospect lists to start his 'Eye Do Photography.' Like that wedding you saw today—I'm sure that bride called me last year, but technically I can't prove she didn't contact Ben more recently." Sandy shook her head and sighed. "Poor suckers. Ben hardly knows how to hold a camera. 'Eye Do Photography.' More like DooDoo Photography."

"Good one, girlfriend!" Bea cackled. She held her fist up for a bump with Sandy's.

"Georgina didn't seem to have much faith in him, either. She handed out disposable digital cameras."

"Huh. Haven't seen those in a while. Glad she had them. That couple should have said 'Eye Don't' to Ben. But the long-and-short of it is, I didn't say a thing about any of this to anyone. I have been careful to make Rhonda think I took the loss in stride."

"That's so unfair!" Angela cried. "I know how hard it is to build those customer lists. You paid for all that marketing, too. Why didn't you fight back?"

Sandy inhaled deeply. "I saw what Rhonda did to Dennis. He tried to stand up for himself, and now she's pushed him to the brink. I don't know how she does it, but somehow she gets people to go along with her nasty ideas. She decides she wants to go after someone, and enough people start withholding referrals or spreading rumors, and it does real damage. I'm not the only one who's careful, who manages—so far—to stay clear. Fiona does. Some of the other old guard, too. But the new vendors seem happy to believe she's in charge. They want those referrals she promises.

They're willing to pay her that commission she expects—and go along with her schemes."

"I knew it!" Bea said. "She's shaking people down. How much?"

"For the record, any vendors paying her commission are doing it voluntarily as far as I know. I don't think it's right, but it's their money. I'm more concerned about what she tells brides—both the good and the bad. Like, obviously, she's telling people Ben is an experienced photographer, when he's not."

"And she did the opposite to poor Dennis?" Angela said.

Sandy nodded. "Remember the DJ at the mixer? Not DJ Tad, the other one—calls himself the Wizard of Weddings? His real name's Cam, and he used to work for Dennis. Dennis employed several DJs and limo drivers back then. He'd built up a solid business over ten or fifteen years. That's hard to do in our industry, but Dennis was tough —hardworking, too. His big dream was to buy an old reception hall downtown and fix it up. He'd even lined up a loan. But then out of the blue, he started losing money. He couldn't figure out why, until his wife figured out that one of his employees was siphoning cash."

"The Wizard of Embezzling?" Bea said.

"You got it. So Dennis—he seems so gruff, but he's really a solid guy, as kind as can be, and he works out a deal that Cam will quit quietly and pay back the money over time. Dennis said he'd keep it all a secret, no police, no charges, as long as Cam made good on paying back the money.

"Truth was, when Dennis let Cam go, a bunch of us in wedding world knew what was what. We knew that Cam had been doing Dennis's books, and then Dennis suddenly decides he won't buy the ballroom, even though he'd been working on it for more than a year. It was easy to put two and two together, but none of us said a peep. Cam seemed sincerely sorry—if that was good enough for Dennis, it was good enough for us.

"But Rhonda had been holding a grudge against Dennis. Long before the thing with Cam happened, Dennis had a spat with Rhonda. He challenged Rhonda—like I said, Dennis can be gruff, and he speaks his mind. And he made the mistake of questioning one of Rhonda's pet projects."

Bea put the last book on the signed pile and handed the pen back to Angela. "Keep going. We're all ears now!"

"Rhonda had it in her head that she was going to put on this big, fancy bridal show. This was when she was still new in town. She had the beginnings of her current entourage, but it was just a few vendors then. To do the show, she had to drum up interest from the rest of us."

"Is that the same thing as a wedding fair?" Angela said. "Where vendors set up exhibits and brides can check out their services?"

Sandy nodded. "Thing was, Dennis had heard a bridal show in Chicago that was this huge scam— we all heard about it, but, you know, Chicago's very far away. We didn't think much of it. But Dennis decided to challenge Rhonda, and honestly, he wasn't polite about it. 'How do we know it won't be a scam like that con in Chicago? None of us really know you, Rhonda.' That kind of thing."

"I bet Rhonda took that in stride—not!" squealed Bea.

"Exactly," Sandy said. "None of the rest of us thought much of it. That's just Dennis's way. He says stuff like that to anyone trying to sell him anything. But Rhonda could hardly hide her rage. She didn't have people under her thumb like she does now, though, so she bit her tongue. But she bided her time until the Cam thing happened, and she saw her chance to retaliate.

"She started telling her crew of vendors how

'unfairly' Dennis treated Cam. She made it her project to help him—as a way to humiliate Dennis. And she got her favorites—by then, she had plenty of them—to jump right in.

"Crazy thing was, Rhonda claimed to be helping Cam, but it was only because of her that people found out what he'd done. She kept saying it was to punish Dennis. But if she hadn't spread all those rumors and gotten her minions to help, the whole thing would have stayed quiet. The story even made it into brides' reviews on wedding sites. Rhonda made things way worse for Cam, even as she promised to help him with referrals."

"She's got the instincts of a gangster," Bea said with a snort. "Cam has to be loyal to her now."

"Yep. He's one more person to do her dirty work. All her little pets know they'd better play along. She whistles, and whatever she wants done is done."

"So do you think she poisoned the salad to get Dennis?" Angela said.

"I don't think so. Why bother? She's already—" Sandy stopped and curled her lips inward, her eyes watering. "She's already brought him down." She looked upward and squeezed her eyes shut for a moment. "And like I said, she doesn't do her own dirty work usually."

"Speaking of Dennis, do you know if he's out of the hospital?" Angela said.

"He's home. I spoke with him just before you got here. Tired but fine, like me. I was worried—especially after you told me that needleweed poisoning can sometimes be fatal. I was sedated and drifting in and out of sleep in the hospital, but at one point I heard lots of beeping and people running to a room near mine. People were yelling out instructions—and then I thought someone said, 'time of death.' I didn't remember it until you told me about the needleweed. I was so relieved that Dennis was fine."

"Sandy, did you happen to see another mixer guest at the hospital? The EMTs brought someone else I didn't meet at the event. An older woman…" Angela said, pausing. "They said she had a heart condition."

"Oh, no," Sandy said. "I didn't see anyone else. Maybe one of the women who worked the check-in desk would know—or maybe Georgina?"

"Speaking of Georgina," Angela said, trying to sound casual, "was she part of Rhonda's plan to bring Dennis down?"

"As far as I know, Georgina only works the

weddings Rhonda's company plans. She's not like the others, who meet with their own prospects every day and can spread bad gossip far and wide. But on the other hand, Rhonda says jump, and Georgina says, 'how high?' It's hard to imagine she wasn't involved in some way."

Angela sighed and looked at Bea. "Shall we head over to Rhonda's? Only fair to hear her side of the story, right?"

"I just texted you the address," Sandy said, tucking her phone back into her pocket. "Have fun visiting her. Don't feel a need to tell her I said hello, though," Sandy said.

"Don't worry, Sandy," Bea said. "Your secrets are safe with us."

As they headed out the door, Bea and Angela promised again to send Sandy the few books she was missing from the *Treacle Town* series. Sandy held the door for them and watched them walk to Angela's car.

"Hey, Sandy," Bea called back from the driveway. "Whatever happened with Rhonda's bridal show?"

"Funny, I never thought about that until just now. Rhonda put it on hold after her little dust-up with Dennis. Said something about the timing not being right, that she wanted to build up her wedding planning business first. Sad, right? All the damage she did to Dennis's business over that bridal show, and she didn't even go through with it in the end."

"Sad is one way of looking at it," Bea said under her breath.

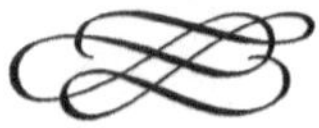

Angela and Bea rang the bell and knocked repeatedly at the front door of Rhonda's riverside bungalow, but no one answered.

"Let's check for a back door," Angela said. "What if her bedroom's in the back? If Rhonda's ill, she might not be able to hear us."

"OK, girlie," Bea said. "Hope springs eternal."

They walked along the driveway to the house's backyard. The shades were drawn, and no light peeked out from the sides. Angela scaled a small staircase to knock on the back door: no answer there, either.

Bea headed in the opposite direction, toward the rear edge of the yard. "I told you! Look!" Bea squealed with delight as she pointed to a large wall of tall weeds. The leaves were by now familiar: needleweed.

"You're right, but can you keep it down?" Angela whispered anxiously. "Since Rhonda's not here, I think what we're doing is technically trespassing."

Angela took out her cell phone and quickly snapped pictures from several angles, including parts of the neighbors' houses and as many other identifying details as possible.

"I've got it. Let's go!" Angela said, urgently beckoning Bea to head back to her car.

"We're not the criminals here. We're catching the criminal."

"It looks that way," Angela said. "Still, I suppose it could still be just a coincidence that Rhonda has needleweed in her yard. It is a weed—"

"You've got a generous imagination, Angie."

"Maybe we've at least got enough for McGregor to investigate now."

Angela settled into the driver's side of her car and reached a hand over to help Bea climb up.

"Thanks, Angie," Bea said. "Is it my imagination, or does this car grow taller as the day goes on?"

"We have made a bunch of stops today," Angela said. "Think of it as a stair workout."

"Good thing, I guess. I didn't get any dancing in today, not even at that wedding reception. DJ Tad says he can get the grannies dancing, but nothing he played got my tootsies tapping. 'Course, he seemed more focused on your pal Georgina than the bride and groom."

"Really? I didn't notice that."

"You don't think they're an item?"

"Hmm. This may be too harsh," Angela started to say. "I think I'll keep my opinion to myself."

"For once, could you please channel the wild-and-crazy Angie who skipped a class or two in college? I deserve a little fun."

"Fine, but I hope you're happy that I'm risking bad karma. Remember, this is just my opinion. You already know how gorgeous Georgina is. Well, I think she always had it in her head—I mean, you know, some beautiful girls, they're... they're almost led to expect, a lifestyle... oh, I don't know how to say it—"

"Spit it out, girlie!" Bea said. "Never mind, I'll say it for you. You'll still have plausible deniability for karma if I guess right. You think Gorgeous George is only gonna give it up for a rich dude. Hot dudes with no dough need not apply, am I right?"

"You make it sound so cynical. But yes, I suppose. In college, she dated the son of a billionaire. His name was Bard something… Bard something the third. Everyone thought they were getting married. All senior year, they said they were 'engaged to be engaged.' But right after graduation, Bard dumped Georgina for a preppy girl he'd known since he was a child. They'd spent every summer together in Maine. She was from one of those rich families that descended from the Mayflower. The society pages called it a matrimonial merger."

"Couldn't Tad be fun on the side? Like she was for Bardie Boy? Until she finds her new Mr. Moneybags?"

"I don't see that happening. Georgina isn't ambitious about much, but finding the right guy—and by 'right,' I mean, you know—"

"Loaded. I get it. So you think she won't bother with a guy just for fun. If you say so, girlie. I still think there might be something there."

"Don't forget, officially, I *didn't* say so." She turned the key in the ignition. "Buckle up, Bea. It's been a long day. I'm looking forward to getting home and seeing Connie and the pups."

"Don't you want to send those pictures to McGregor before we go?"

"Not right now. I'll do it when we get home, so

that I can include all the links I can find about needleweed poisoning and explain that Fiona identified the leaves for us. I don't want to give him an excuse to brush me off again. That reminds me," she said, rifling through her purse, "I think I must have left those leaves at Fiona's. Ugh."

"Should we go back and get them?"

"It's at least forty minutes in the wrong direction," Angela said glumly. "I'll just text Fiona now and tell her to hold onto the bag in case McGregor needs it for evidence."

ASEEM LOOKED AT THE LITTLE BAG OF LEAVES ON the passenger side of his car and sighed. It felt good to have something to do—something that, hopefully, would get Angela talking to him again. Something he could do to help.

As he drove west down the freeway toward Sacramento, he replayed the crazy highs and lows of the day. Between himself and Angela, he wasn't usually the excitable one. That was one of the reasons they were well-matched. They balanced each other out.

Angela sometimes let her feelings get the

better of her, while he was slow to react—sometimes to a fault.

But he hadn't been slow to react today. Not hardly.

Watching Angela—Angel—drive away crying, furious at him, was much too much to take in stride.

And only minutes before, he'd been on the high of his life! His career idol hadn't just praised his ideas, hadn't just wanted to back him, but wanted him to lead a portfolio of startups. A completely unexpected thrill—until Gary said too many of the wrong things to Angela.

Aseem chided himself that it was his own fault. Gary said too much because he, Aseem, had confessed too much. He felt grateful Fiona had been there to calm him down.

"Come inside, breathe a minute. Let me make you a cup of tea," Fiona had said kindly. She'd deftly interrupted when Aseem began to lose his temper with Gary. She'd instantly conjured an errand for her husband, delicately sending him away without hurting his feelings. Gary hadn't even noticed he was being handled—or rather, taken care of, with love.

Gary leads a company worth billions. Lucky for Gary, Fiona leads him.

The thought brought a smile to Aseem's face. Truth was, maybe Gary—Awkward Gary—hadn't gotten it all wrong about him and Angela.

Because isn't what Gary and Fiona have exactly what Angela and I want?

At the big farmhouse table, Fiona had poured him a cup of Earl Grey from a pretty porcelain pot.

"One sec," she said, opening a cabinet under the kitchen island and pulling out a bottle of Heavenly Mash whiskey. "Just a splash. Bourbon's one of the best American things," Fiona said. "Just don't tell my mum's Scottish relatives."

It made Aseem smile that the bourbon was Connie's family's brand. He sipped the tea while Fiona asked tactful questions and shared gentle advice.

"A few fights are normal, aren't they? If you've had none so far, perhaps you were overdue? In my estimation, it's part of becoming more committed. Fighting fair is what's important."

Fiona's way was so soothing. Especially her accent. It reminded Aseem of his mother's obsession with BBC America.

"Of course," Fiona had continued, "you both must know what you want, and be honest about it. Have you been?"

Aseem found himself half-nodding. He cautiously recapped for Fiona what he'd told Gary. He tried to be more precise as he described his dreams of being part of a startup—careful not to short-change how much he enjoyed working side-by-side with Angela and supporting her vision, while also being realistic about his own aspirations for the future.

"Don't mind Gary if he got it a bit wrong, Aseem. My husband sees the world as a collection of problems to solve—and as we both know, he solves many. I can't help but love that he sees our experience as something he's proud of, but maybe he projects a bit more than he should onto others. You should be honest with him about what you'd like in your working relationship, too."

Aseem reached the bottom of the tea, and a restored equilibrium, just as Gary returned. She greeted him with a hug and a kiss, and suggested that he and Aseem might have something to talk about.

"I agree!" Gary said, all optimistic energy. "Let's figure out how we're going to do great things together!" Aseem nodded and followed Gary out the huge glass sliding doors to walk the grounds and discuss how their grand plans would unfurl. Aseem looked back tentatively at Fiona, who mouthed, "It's all right," and pointed at her heart. "Truth."

An hour later, they returned to the farmhouse, all smiles. Aseem said his goodbyes.

"May I ask you to bring this to Angela?" Fiona asked. "She left it here, and I think she might need it."

"Of course. What is it?"

Fiona explained that Angela had found the plant and that it appeared to be what had poisoned the mixer guests, and that she, Angela, and Bea had discussed who might have a motive to do it.

"She didn't mention that to me," Aseem said. "Maybe if she starts speaking to me again, I can point out I wasn't the only one with a secret."

"You mean *when* she starts speaking to you, right?"

"Thank you—when. I can't help be curious, though—did you, Angela, and Bea discuss any suspects in particular?"

"Rhonda, naturally. Bea's nearly certain. Angela's more inclined to give Rhonda the benefit of the doubt."

"Of course she is," Aseem said. "Did they consider the caterers? They had full access to the kitchen, which the poisoner would have needed, and, of course, they prepared all the salads and other foods. Is that too obvious?"

"I'm no Miss Marple," Fiona said, "but that might be my first guess. I can't imagine what Paige and her crew would have for a motive, though. If people get poisoned by her food, that could be ruinous for her business, I'd imagine."

"Georgina and the others readily assumed the inn was to blame. Would Paige have known they'd do that? Could she have counted on it?"

"Kind of a high-risk game, wouldn't you say?"

"Good point. But then, that makes me wonder, could the poisoner have been trying to hurt Paige's reputation? Maybe that was the motive."

"I suppose it's possible. Would you like to try to talk with Paige, since you've already come all this way? I know the event she's catering tonight. I did the flowers and my assistant is delivering them. You could try to catch her at her commissary kitchen—I'm sure she'll be stopping there between events—or at the country club where she'll be setting up in a couple of hours."

Fiona wrote the two addresses on a slip of paper and handed it to Aseem, who seemed immediately more motivated and upbeat.

"I don't know that I've ever pleased anyone as

much with a couple of addresses," Fiona said, smiling.

"Might sound silly, but if I could figure this out for Angel—"

"He's fighting for the honor of his woman, Fee. Chivalry is not dead!" Gary said, accompanying his comment with a melodramatic impression of a knight bowing with an imaginary sword and dropping to one knee. But on his way down, he lost his balance and fell over on one shoulder, clunking his temple on the floor.

"Are you all right, darling?" Fiona said, rushing to his side.

"I'm fine, just a little embarrassed," Gary laughed. "Awkward Gary strikes again!"

❧

ANGELA TURNED HER CAR AWAY FROM RHONDA'S house and back toward the freeway and sighed. "Still want pizza on the way back?"

"You sound like you're hoping I don't," Bea said with a cackle. "Now I'm unsure of how I should answer."

"I wonder if they have drive-through. A promise is a promise, so we'll get pizza if you want, but is it OK if we don't eat it there?"

"No worries, Angie. Drive-through is just fine."

It only took them a few minutes to reach the wide boulevard that would take them back to the freeway. As Angela was about to round the curve, Bea shouted, "Weren't we just speaking of the devil?"

A large van was heading toward them, covered all over in familiar branding that shouted "Get Granny Dancing!"

"Angie, isn't that Gorgeous George in the passenger seat?"

Without stopping to think, Angela sped toward the first U-turn lane. While she waited for the light to turn, she noticed Bea's expression and headed off her question. "I'm just thinking—OK, I don't know what I'm thinking. I guess if they're going to check on Rhonda, maybe they'll know where she could be. Maybe they'll know why— you know—"

"Why she poisoned people at the mixer? I can get behind that thinkin', girlie."

They sped around the bend and Bea spotted a parking space a house away from Rhonda's. Georgina and Tad were already out of the van and walking toward Rhonda's door. "Park here, Angie. Let's hide and watch what they do for a minute."

"So suspicious, Bea," Angie complained, but

she followed Bea's advice and slipped her car into the inconspicuous spot. Bea rolled down her window to listen in, and Angela leaned toward Bea for a better view. They watched Tad jog around to the backyard, despite Georgina saying, "Wait a second while I check!" as she climbed the front steps and peered into the windows.

In a flash, Tad ran back from the rear of the house toward Georgina. "I've got it, babe! No need to worry." He had a small pair of thick, sturdy scissors, the handle coated in bright blue plastic. He had threaded his index finger through one loop of the handle and was spinning the tool delightedly.

"'Babe'—did you hear that, Angie?"

"Shhh! They'll hear us," Angela whispered. "But yes, I heard."

They watched as Georgina took one of her white gloves out of her pocket and put it on, then opened her purse.

"Whoa," Angela hissed, noticing the redness on her friend's hands, even from the distance of the car. "That poison ivy of hers is really something."

"Or something else," Bea muttered.

With her gloved hand, Georgina delicately took the shears from Tad and dropped them in her large purse. "Let's get out of here," she said urgently as she zipped the top of her bag.

"That's our cue, Angie," Bea said, opening her door and hopping out, calling out to Georgina in her most sing-songy old lady voice. "Oh, Georgina—hello there, dear."

Angela jumped out of her side and joined Bea in approaching Georgina and Tad. "George—Georgina, I mean—how are you?"

"Angela! What—what are you doing here?"

"Sorry to sneak up on you," Angela said. "We just came to check on Rhonda. Since we were up here to observe your wedding, we stopped at Sandy Givens' place to see how she was doing since leaving the hospital and so Bea could sign her collection of Treacle Town books. We told her we were worried that Rhonda might have gotten ill, too, and Sandy gave us the address so we could check on her."

"Yes—us, too," Georgina said quickly. "Tad and I finished up the wedding downtown a little while ago—well, you know that, of course—and since we hadn't heard from Rhonda, we came by to check on her, too. If anyone can take care of herself, it's Rhonda. But it's not like her to be out of touch. To be honest, I'm a little worried, too."

"Guess Rhonda's not here, then?" Bea said. Georgina nodded.

"You weren't kidding about the poison ivy," Angela said, looking closely at Georgina's ungloved hand. "My goodness, that looks horrible!" Georgina hastily shoved it into her pocket.

"You know how it is with rashes. They always look worse than they are," Georgina insisted. "It's practically gone now." She pulled the second glove out of her pocket and put it on her bare hand. "I took my gloves off after the wedding to give it some air. I didn't think I'd run into anyone. That's better. No one wants to see a rashy hand, right?"

"Do you do gardening work for Rhonda, too?" Bea said, in her treacliest, least threatening tone. "I noticed the garden scissors you put in your purse."

"Those aren't hers," Tad interrupted. "Rhonda asked us to look for them."

Georgina looked alarmed, then piped up before Tad could continue. "Great eye, Bea. I do help Rhonda with her gardening sometimes. She's got a lovely yard, and we've been brainstorming what to plant after getting rid of some of the old plants. Some of them look pretty, but anything's a weed if it's not what you want, Rhonda says.

"I remembered during the wedding that I had left the shears out. I just thought that we could kill two birds with one stone—check on Rhonda and retrieve the shears. I wouldn't want them to get wet. What if it rains? Garden tools rust so easily."

"So true, dear," Bea said.

Angela curled her lips inside her mouth and looked slightly to the side, her eyes trained on the small wooden structure at the end of Rhonda's driveway. Was it an old-fashioned stand-alone garage, or was it a garden shed?

"Angela, I see you're looking at the shed," Georgina said. "It's locked, and I don't have the key. That's why I'm taking the shears with me—in case you're wondering."

"Not at all," Angela said. "My mind was just wandering. You said something about rain, and it made me wonder if I'm supposed to cover up the chicken coop. Bea, I think we'd better head back to Napa."

"Of course, Angie," Bea said, winking at Angela once her back was to Georgina and Tad.

"Look at the time! We'd better get going, too," Georgina said, pointing to the watch on Tad's wrist. "Tad's got another wedding this evening. C'mon, Tad, let's hurry." The two of them hustled to Tad's van, and were hopping in when Bea turned around and yelled back at them, "You'll tell

Rhonda we were concerned about her when you see her, won't you?"

Angela chimed in, "Oh yes—Georgina, you will let us know that she's OK when you hear from her, won't you?"

"You'll be the first to know," Georgina said, smiling and waving from the passenger side window. "Bye now!"

"Take your time, Bea," Angela said under her breath as she opened the passenger side door and offered Bea a hand. "I want to watch them drive off." As Tad's van zoomed by, both he and Georgina waved enthusiastically, exaggerated grins plastered on their faces. Angela responded in kind.

"Great day so far," Angela said, scowling. "Lied to by two people I trusted in one day. At least I can hand McGregor more evidence."

"Wait, so you're not giving Georgina the benefit of the doubt?" Bea said.

"No need to mock me, Bea. Even I'm not that naïve. She's worried about it raining? Just for laughs, I'm going to do a web search to see how many times in history it's rained on this date in Sacramento. Especially when the air's dry as a bone and the sky is as blue as can be. No, my dear old friend is definitely lying. Too much of that going around today."

"I can't believe I'm coming to Georgina's defense, but we've heard all day how threatening Rhonda can be. Maybe she just had Georgina pull the needleweed for her, and Georgina didn't even know what for. Or even if Georgina did know, this was probably not the first time Rhonda used Georgina as a henchman. Maybe Georgina felt she couldn't refuse."

"It's sinking pretty low when you can't refuse to poison people, Bea. I'll be as cynical as you are before too long if this keeps up. I just wish I hadn't left that bag of leaves at Fiona's," Angela said, putting her phone in the cradle and tapping it for directions. "I'd feel better if I could hand that to McGregor, too. Should I ask Fiona to mail it to us?"

"Don't worry about that. Assuming McGregor takes on the case, I'm guessing he can get a local sheriff to help him out. They can send someone to pick up the evidence."

The phone rang, and Angela smiled a little. "Hi, Connie. It's nice to see a friendly face. We are just about to head home."

"I thought you could use a little cheering up," Connie said. "The pups and I are heading up to my place to pull the tarp off that car. I thought you'd enjoy seeing how well-behaved they are. I'm going to let them run beside the stroller on the way up. They're really learning to respond to commands, and they can walk further now, too."

Connie turned the camera on her phone around so that Angela and Bea could see the adorable parade of four little dachshunds bouncing alongside the stroller on the walkway from the inn to the barn and the trail to Heavenly West. The light from the setting sun was soft and warm. Bijou was along for the walk, too, looking surprisingly sedate in comparison to her little ones.

"They are adorable," Angela said. "Thank you for showing me. It's like a tonic."

"This way, Dames. Over here, Paprika," Connie said. The little troop rounded the bend near the barn, and Dames and Paprika started to look bolder and more curious. "C'mon, you two. Why can't you be more like your brother and sister?"

As Connie pushed the stroller past the barn and toward the chicken coop, the two mischievous pups spotted something and ran for it, suddenly oblivious to Connie's urgent instructions. "Oh—wait, Dames, no! The chickens!"

Connie hastily dropped her phone on the trail,

so Bea and Angela could see only Connie's arm and snippets of canine legs and tails as Connie hastily scooped up Garnet and Jonathan and plopped them into the stroller. "Bijou, not you, too! Please don't hurt the chickens!"

CHAPTER 13

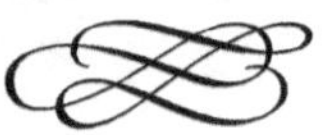

Angela could hear Connie's shoes on the gravel trail as she ran to stop the dogs from hurting the birds. Angela yelled into her phone that there was no need to worry—she'd kept the coop, but the rental company had picked the chickens up the day before. But Connie was so focused on stopping Dames and Paprika, nothing Angela said registered.

"What is that, Dames? Put that down! Oh no, it's a chicken bone!"

Bea started to snicker. "Now that's funny. I hope it wasn't one of your pet chickens, Angela."

"Nope, they were all accounted for when the rental company picked them up yesterday. Bones and all."

They saw the bottom of Connie's elbow swing past the screen as she lifted the two runaway puppies into the stroller with their siblings. Connie picked up the phone and looked into the camera. "So much for that experiment. I guess we'll be on our way with all the little ones on the pushcart. C'mon, Bijou. Time to go," Connie laughed. "Oh Angela, you can't see it, but now Bijou's trying to wedge her nose inside a crack in the barn door."

"She's fascinated by that barn," Angela said. "I don't like her odds of moving that door."

Then Bijou started to yelp and cry, and Connie stuck the phone in her pocket as she ran to see what was wrong.

"Sounds like Bijou got her snout stuck," Angela sighed. "Again."

"This movie's getting less interesting," Bea said.

Angela tapped the mute button. "Don't tell Connie, but I agree." She tipped her head backward and rolled it around on her shoulders. "The puppies are cute and all, but I think we'd better hit the road. It's going to be dark soon. Do you think she'd understand if we hung up?" Angela sighed. "Maybe we should wait a minute longer."

She leaned her head against the car window, patiently listening to the muffled sounds of Connie telling Bijou to wait a minute so that she could open the big barn door and get her unstuck. Bijou stopped crying, apparently freed from the door. But then after a beat came Connie's panicked shriek, and Angela and Bea both sat bolt upright in their seats.

"Connie! Connie, are you OK?!" Angela yelled into the phone, not remembering that she'd put the microphone on mute. "Connie! What's happening?"

Angela and Bea both leaned closer to the phone, trying to hear Connie's response, but all they could hear was a faint sound of her crying in the distance. Then the crying grew closer, and they heard the sound of Connie's shoes crunching on the path.

Connie picked up the phone and looked into the camera, her face white with shock and damp with tears. "Angela, are you still there? It's awful— it's—I'll show you."

Then she walked back into the barn, her phone's camera capturing each step. Inside the barn door, they could see Bijou nosing around the oversized wine cask that had doubled as a table. The cask was no longer standing upright, but was slightly tilted, one side propped by something sticking out from under and inside. As Connie homed in on it with her phone's camera,

Bea and Angela could plainly see what it was: a , bloated human foot, straining the confines of its sensible shoe. The rest of the body it was attached to appeared to be shoved up inside the cask.

"Oh, boy," Bea said. "I know whose shoe that is."

"Me, too," Angela muttered, hand over her mouth.

"I guess you were right after all, girlie. Rhonda definitely does not look well."

"Angela, can you hear me?" Connie was saying. "Are you there?"

Angela remembered the mute button and gave it a tap. "Yes, I'm here, Connie. I'm sorry—"

"Tell me what to do. That big cask is awfully heavy, but should I try to move it to see who's under it? Should I see if she could be… alive?" Connie gulped audibly as she said it.

"Good idea. Just tip the barrel over and make a run for it. I'm guessing Rhonda's going to be pretty mad!" Bea cackled.

"Bea!" Angela said, frowning. "Connie, ignore that comment. Bea likes to joke inappropriately when she's upset, don't you, Bea? It's easier than dealing with feelings."

"Oh, yes," Bea said, putting the back of her

hand on her forehead melodramatically. "I'm beside myself with emotion."

"Seriously, Connie, don't move anything. If you don't mind, go to the front desk and ask Jackson to call the police and ask for Sergeant McGregor. Tell him what happened. He'll know what to do. And tell him we'll be back in a little over an hour—and we have more evidence for him."

"Will do," Connie said, exhaling heavily. "Bea, are you sure it's Rhonda? Based on one foot?"

"Sadly, yes. Unfortunately, that means our big dreams of becoming a Wine Country wedding factory may be on hold. Sorry, Angie," Bea said, with another inappropriate chuckle, earning another cluck of the tongue from Angela. "Look on the bright side, though, Connie. I'm pretty sure we know whose vehicle's stashed in your half-built garage."

A FEW HOURS LATER, ANGELA, BEA, AND CONNIE gathered in Angela's suite. The door adjoining Connie's suite was open, and Bijou and her puppies were wandering in and out as they pleased. Connie and Bea were seated in front of a small table near the window on two puffy chairs, both upholstered in a cheerful pattern of holly leaves and berries on a white background. Connie had just refilled a big bowl with cheddar-cheese popcorn and put it back on the table.

"After a day like today, it's a relief to be immersed in Christmas again," Angela said, plopping down on the red and green quilt on top of her bed. "I can almost forget that it's springtime, and that we just spent the last hour dealing with Sergeant McGregor—and that he'll be back tomorrow to question us again."

"Not to mention that dead body," Connie said, wincing as she pulled the cork from a second bottle of wine. "I think I'm still traumatized—and all I really saw was her foot."

Bea chuckled with her mouth full of popcorn, causing a few bits to stray from the side of her mouth. "Maybe it was viewing it through the cell phone, but I thought it was kind of funny. With her foot sticking out from that barrel, Rhonda was like a low-rent Wicked Witch of the West."

"Technically," Angela said, "she'd have to be a low-rent Wicked Witch of the *East*. That's the one that had the house dropped on her."

"She can't be the Wicked Witch of the East.

That's what Pat called not-so-dearly departed Babs."

Babs—aka Barbara Devereaux—was the former owner of the winery property Connie had turned into Heavenly West. Barbara Devereaux had moved from the East Coast to California after selling her publishing house, a company she'd built in a cutthroat fashion that left destruction and tears in her wake. Before she died, she'd been in the process of turning around Domaine Devereaux, her husband's failing winery, using the same combination of business smarts, determination, and ruthlessness—in the process, creating new enemies who weren't sad to see her go.

Connie giggled as she refreshed all three of their wine glasses. "I'm feeling a little bad about giving you that leftover cask from Domaine Devereaux. Turning it into that tall table seemed like such a lovely way to re-purpose it for your barn. Who could have predicted someone would try to hide a dead body with it? Gives me an idea for a Halloween party, though. If only she'd had a striped sock on that over-inflated foot of hers—"

"And a pretty red shoe instead of that prison matron special," Bea snickered. "Even I'm more fashionable than Rhonda."

Angela snorted and almost spat out her wine. "Wait, what?"

The three of them laughed heartily and clinked their glasses together. "Thanks for this, Connie. Feels good to laugh after today. Two betrayals and a dead body—surely that's some kind of individual record for a bad day."

"While I enjoy the sarcasm, Angie, I remind you that you promised to give Aseem a chance to explain," Bea said. "I don't believe he betrayed you. My money's still on Gary garbling the message."

"And you also promised to tell me what's going on. I don't even know who Gary is," Connie said.

"Let's just decompress for a bit longer," Angela said. "Besides, even if—and it's a big if—Aseem didn't really lie to me and go looking for a new job—oh, brother, you two have already got me talking about it. Anyway, it's obviously a very big if, because we know at least one part of that did happen. He definitely lied to me. He told me he was going to Silicon Valley, and instead we find him at Fiona's in Playfair Pines.

"And Bea, even setting Aseem's behavior aside, surely you'd agree that getting betrayed by my dear old friend George is bad enough for one day. And now to think she's also a murderer!"

"You're really sure she did it?" Connie said.

"She had the motive," Angela said.

"So did half the wedding industry," Bea said. "Maybe more than half."

"You're forgetting that we caught her red-handed—literally—in a garden full of needleweed. Holding the shears. And that 'poison ivy' of hers—I haven't had a chance to research yet, but I'd be willing to bet that's what happens when you handle needleweed without gloves. I say we can be sure, at a minimum, that she was our poisoner." Angela started to tear up. "She's really not the Georgina I used to know, I guess. I mean, she always liked her shortcuts, but I could never imagine her poisoning anybody, much less murdering someone."

"Even if she did do the poisoning, that doesn't mean she murdered Rhonda, though, does it?" Connie asked gently.

"I think she wanted to frame Rhonda for the poisoning, and Rhonda caught on. I think she was hoping that Rhonda would go to jail—or maybe just be discredited, I don't know. Thinking things through and doing them the right way wasn't Georgina's strong suit, at least not when the right way was harder. Like I said, she was always after a shortcut."

"Do you think Rhonda confronted her in the

barn, Angie? And then Georgina killed her to avoid getting caught for the poisoning?"

"Something like that. My guess is a crime of passion, of sorts. You noticed how Georgina was under Rhonda's thumb, even more than everybody else was. I think she just snapped. She'd never get where she wanted to go being Rhonda's flunkie." Angela dabbed at her eyes with a napkin and calmed herself.

"You're making me feel sorry for her, even if she did do it," Bea said. "She was practically an indentured servant. Still, are you sure she's strong enough to drag Rhonda under that cask? Just lifting one side of the cask would be hard for one person—and Georgina doesn't strike me as the weightlifting type. Not to mention that Rhonda was no lightweight."

"The barrel's not as heavy as it looks. The bottom was removed, don't forget. I think she could have set the barrel on its side, shoved Rhonda in, then tipped it back up. She could have used the post holding up the hayloft for leverage. Plus, adrenaline gives you strength—I'm sure that fear of getting caught murdering someone gives you a good shot of adrenaline," Angela said drolly.

"What was the timing? During the middle of the mixer?"

"Yep. No witnesses, because everyone else was inside networking. And you remember how nervous Georgina seemed doing the announcements in Rhonda's place. Remember how I thought— silly me—that it might have been stage fright? You're sure right about me being too trusting, Bea."

"Don't be too hard on yourself. I hardly trust anybody, and even I usually have trouble believing someone's a murderer! I still think we're missing a few pieces of this puzzle. Are you assuming Rhonda found the needleweed in the same place you did, in the kitchen? The little bag on the floor?"

"Yes, I think she must have found it in the kitchen. But there were probably several bags— they would have needed a lot of it to poison that many people. I figure Georgina cleaned them all up, but missed the one I found because it fell behind the trash. Shoot, that reminds me, I wish I hadn't left that bag of needleweed leaves at Fiona's. I should email her to tell her McGregor will ask her about it. Do you mind?"

Angela clicked the power button on her laptop and sat down at her desk. "It will only take a second. Oh wait—I guess that means I have to tell Fiona about Rhonda. I need to think about this.

Should I call her in the morning? How do we tell people Rhonda's dead?"

"I've got an idea," Bea said deviously, hopping down from her chair. "Hit the record button on your phone." Then Bea marched around the room doing her best imitation of a marching munchkin, singing "Ding Dong! The Witch Is Dead." "C'mon, Connie, sing it with me!"

"Not exactly tasteful, Bea," Angela said.

Angela's computer chimed and she turned back to it. "Oh great! The perfect icing on the catastrophic cake today has been. Look at this alert." She pushed her chair back, inviting Bea and Connie to read the email on her computer screen. "Someone's written an article about the poisoning at the mixer. It's on the *Wine Country Grapevine*. Lexie—I knew I couldn't trust her!"

"Angie, I don't think it's Lexie," Bea said. "The title is *Food-Borne Illness Outbreak at Beloved Local Inn: Can Betty Snickerdoodle's Reputation Be Saved?* Lexie's the one who told us that most food-borne illness doesn't come on that fast."

Angela clicked the link and pulled the article up on her computer. Sure enough, the byline wasn't Lexie's. The article was credited to the editor. Angela sighed. "Maybe you're right, Bea. Lexie's boss is shown as the author."

"I bet Lexie refused to write it and her editor took over. You know how desperate the *Grapevine* is to attract attention," Connie said.

"It's been a long day, Angie. I'm going to my room," Bea said, hopping up from her chair. Her perky expression was out of sync with her words. "May I make a suggestion? Why not let McGregor tell Fiona what happened? It's his job, and we already know he doesn't do much, so why take this task that you don't want to do off his plate? Besides, you already texted Fiona to tell her not to throw out the leaves. The rest can wait. Call her in the morning if you want to. Try to relax a little tonight."

Angela frowned. "Yeah, but what about that article? I should respond somehow."

"Nothing to be done about that tonight, either," Bea said quickly. "I'm convinced everything will look better in the morning," she added, before closing the door behind her.

"She's right, Angela," Connie said kindly. "Have a seat with me at the table. Weren't we supposed to have girl talk tonight?"

"You're right. I can get a little obsessive," Angela said, smiling just a little. She pulled up the empty chair and grabbed a handful of popcorn.

"Was it just me, or did it seem like Bea was in a hurry?"

"It wasn't just you. For someone saying she'd had a long day, she was moving like green grass through a goose."

"I don't know exactly what you mean, Connie. But I think I'm glad the rental company picked up that goose."

"Rebecca, call Lexie Greene," Bea commanded the tubular internet device. Within a moment, Lexie answered.

"This is a surprise," Lexie said.

"So was that hit piece on your website, Hot Pants."

"Ouch. I know. It just published half an hour ago. I was planning to call Angela in the morning. It wasn't my doing—"

"We saw that your boss took the credit. I'm not sure Angela's convinced you're not involved."

"The person who sent me the lead about the wave of illness at the inn must have been disappointed that I didn't jump on the story. She emailed the main tip box on our website—that's how our editor got wind of it. That box sends copies to everyone on the staff. I tried to stop it. Had to tread carefully, of course. My boss wasn't persuaded by my concerns about getting the facts wrong."

"She? You're sure the tipster was a she?"

"Maybe you haven't read the story yet. I've got a pretty good hunch who the 'anonymous source' is. She describes herself as a 'Northern California wedding planner'—"

"Anyone could say that in an email."

"True. But the source emailed me directly using a disposable email account."

"Disposable email?"

"An email address that you can't reply to. People use it legitimately to avoid receiving un-wanted mail—or illegitimately to send it."

"Someone had to be smart and devious enough to know about that."

"Yes. And more important in this case, only three people at your mixer had my personal email address."

"Rats. I'm guessing Rhonda wasn't one of them."

"Nope. You sound disappointed."

"Bad read, I guess. I really thought Rhonda was the culprit. It would be better for Angie if it wasn't her old pal doing the sabotage, but now the smart money's gotta be on Georgina."

"We don't know why, though—Rhonda had Georgina on an awfully short leash at that photo shoot. Maybe she was following Rhonda's orders."

"Speaking of Rhonda, I should have mentioned she's dead. I think this might be what you journos call 'burying the lede.'"

"Textbook example," Lexie laughed. "No offense, but hard to imagine you're sad about it. Is it a bummer or not?"

"She was kind of fun to play with, so I say yeah, bummer," Bea chuckled. "Oops—buried it again. Ol' Rhonda didn't just die, it's pretty clear ol' Rhonda was murdered—right here at the inn. Definite bummer for her—but maybe it's an opportunity for you and me." Then she shared the basics of how Connie found the body in the barn.

"It's good news for me, since I'll be back on the crime beat again, though I must say, my brief stint in the land of veils and bouquets has been less boring than I expected. And don't worry, I'll be fair to the inn in my coverage."

"I'm not worried about that. And since you'll be following in Sergeant McGregor's footsteps now, you're not going to be testing any speed records. He thinks it's solved already, and if he's wrong, who knows how long it'll take him to cotton on? In the meantime, I've got an idea we can work on together, if you're interested. I think it's a lot more exciting—especially since you've taken a shine to the wedding world."

Bea told Lexie her idea for a project exploring the dark side of the wedding industry. It had been bubbling in the back of her mind since Sandy Givens told her about the big bridal fair scam in Chicago—and how the culprits were never caught, and how it cast a shadow over the wedding industry as far away as Sacramento.

"Who knows? Maybe you'll even solve the mystery of the bridal fair scammer. Even if not, I'm thinking maybe you get an exposé to add to your clippings, and if you learn anything extra juicy, I get a fun angle for my next mystery. I bet you'll find all kinds of dirt when you start looking into the wedding fair thing. And you've already got Rhonda's knee-breaker networking approach in your hip pocket as another delicious anecdote from the dark side. I think this could be a big deal. If the exposé's exciting enough, maybe you'll get national attention."

"Count me in," Lexie said. "My Pulitzer quest starts in the morning."

"I like a girl who thinks big."

"Occupational requirement for journalism.

Shrinking violets need not apply. Thanks for thinking of me, Bea. Not to get all mushy about it, but it's kind of an honor, teaming up with a best-selling author."

"Oh, brother. The last thing I need is another person kissing my backside. Don't get over-excited about working with me until you've tried it —you might not even like it," Bea said, followed by one of her signature cackles. "I think that the wedding fair scandal is a great place to start. If you dig up anything fresh along the way, you'll let me know, right?"

"I will. A freelancer friend of mine used to work for a Chicago paper. He's in Florida now, but maybe he remembers something or someone. I'll see if he can give me a shove in the right direction. Since I have to cover her murder anyway, I love the idea of making Rhonda's protection racket part of the exposé, too. She's dead, so she can't complain. And if I look into both at the same time, I can get the *Grapevine* to cover some of my expenses for digging into her racket."

"Like the way you think, hotshot. Of course, I want to hear anything you uncover about the dearly departed, too."

Lexie hung up and Bea headed into the bathroom to brush her teeth and get ready for bed.

"This is something new," she said, holding up a charmingly packaged, Betty Snickerdoodle-branded tube of toothpaste. "It's almost too pretty to use." She squirted a blob of green and red gel onto her toothbrush, put the brush in her mouth, and began to laugh. "Gingerbread-mint toothpaste! Angie girl, what will you think of next?"

Bea changed into one of her ancient nighties and climbed into her bed. But as soon as she shut off the light, she remembered there was one more call she needed to make, to a person who might know the answer to an important question about Rhonda's murder. She was so tired, though, it would have to wait until tomorrow.

"Rebecca," Bea said loudly. "Remind me to call Pat Rogers in the morning."

"Reminder set," cooed the voice from the tube.

ASEEM KNOCKED SOFTLY ON ANGELA'S DOOR—so softly, it was easy to ignore at first.

"Angel, I know it's late, but I can tell you're up. Can I talk to you for a minute?"

"He sounds sad, honey," Connie said after the third knock. Angela had just told her why she was so upset with Aseem. Like Bea, Connie was sure there was a misunderstanding at the heart of the matter, though she hadn't shared that opinion with Angela. As she saw it, her role was to be a good listener—and perhaps offer the gentlest of nudges when the right opportunity presented itself. "You sure you don't want to answer?"

"I'm sure. But you could answer. Not from here—go through to your suite and talk to him from your door."

Connie sighed and complied. She opened her suite door and told Aseem that Angela wasn't up for talking to him right now.

"Can you give her this?" Aseem said, holding out the bag of leaves Angela had left at Fiona's farm. "Fiona asked me to deliver them. And tell her… tell her Fiona told me about the poison, and I had a theory of my own. I got a little information on the caterers—probably a dead end, but it could help eliminate some possibilities. Tell her—tell her I'll be happy to fill her in when she's ready to talk to me."

"I will," Connie said, heading back into her suite as Aseem walked away. But then she stopped and hurried after him. "I'm sure she'll come around," Connie whispered. "Don't worry."

CHAPTER 14

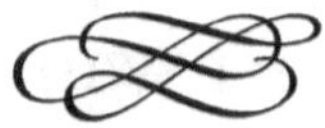

The next morning, Bea and Angela were sitting on Bea's little bench, savoring the light breeze and a quiet breakfast of coffee and egg sandwiches. They were waiting for Sergeant McGregor and his junior officer, who were due to arrive soon for a detailed examination of the spot where Rhonda's body was found. Angela still looked tired from the long day before, but she'd managed a quick, neat outfit of jeans and a long-sleeved t-shirt. Bea was still wearing her nightie and robe on top of velour sweatpants, the tip of her velcro sneakers barely touching the ground.

"It's McGregor," said the voice on the speaker of Angela's cell. "Change of plans. Short-handed today. I had to send Officer Carroll up to Sacramento to bring Georgina Peterson in, and Officer Babiak was already committed to a detail at the craft fair on Main Street today. Small town police problems. We won't be over to your crime scene until later this afternoon. This is awkward—but can I count on you to make sure no one touches anything?"

"Sure," Angela said. "Shouldn't be a problem, since you taped it off—"

"We could hire Pat Rogers to guard it for you," Bea said. "I'm pretty sure she's available. She's got a uniform, and her rate's quite reasonable."

"Sickles!" McGregor said. "Butting in again. Shocker."

"Sorry, Sergeant. I should have told you we were on speakerphone," Angela said.

McGregor let out a sound that was part sigh, part grunt. "I suppose that's not a bad idea, Beatrice. We pay minimum wage plus $2. Pat can like it or lump it."

Bea's nose crinkled slightly at "Beatrice." McGregor had an annoying habit of calling her by the name she hadn't heard from anyone else—by choice—in nearly sixty years. "With generous wages like that, it's hard to imagine why you're short-handed. But I bet I can persuade her."

"Cute, Sickles. Angela, we're working with

local law enforcement up in Sac to let potential witnesses know we'll need to speak with them. Can I get a list of contacts who were at the event from you?"

"Not a complete list. Rhonda managed everything herself. But Bea and I can put our heads together and jot down everyone we remember. I think you'll find most of their contact info online easily—they've all got websites. One of the photographers, Sandy Givens, took pictures, too. You might want to talk with her first."

"Thanks for the tip. Send the list as soon as you can. Oh, and can you let Connie Hollander know that we may not get to examining the deceased's vehicle for another couple of days? I know the garage has no door yet, but ask her to do her best to keep the vehicle secure."

"Will do. Connie already parked her own car behind Rhonda's to prevent anyone from moving it."

McGregor hung up and Angela got up from the bench and yawned and stretched. "If I'd known he wasn't coming, I would have slept in. I suppose it's not so bad to have the morning free. I still need to figure out what to do about that *Grapevine* article. Assuming you're right, and

Lexie wasn't involved, do you think she might help me with the fallout?"

"Can't hurt to ask. While you talk to Lexie, I'll go to my suite and call Pat. But first, how about you and I take our own little peek at the crime scene?"

"We just promised McGregor we would keep everyone away from it."

"I'm sure he meant everyone *else*. And if not, that's definitely what *we* meant, right?"

"Fine. What are we looking for?"

"Anything McGregor might miss. You heard him say he's short-handed again. You know he told me last winter that he didn't mind me helping."

"That was before the last two murders here at the inn. Don't you think he's changed his tune? And I know you're really thinking one of two things: that you'll solve the crime first and show McGregor up, or you'll get an idea for your next mystery story. Scratch that: you're thinking both."

"Even if those things are true, Angie," Bea said innocently, "don't you think it's a good idea for us to gather a little evidence of our own? Maybe get a few pictures on that phone of yours, just for backup? McGregor will have at most one cop helping him—and he's not that sharp even with a full team. And are you forgetting that he refused to even look into the poisoning? He's not exactly a perfectionist!"

Angela could hardly deny that McGregor's approach was sometimes a little...bumbling. "No reason fighting the public relations fire can't wait a little longer. If nothing else, it's nice to get a little more morning air."

The two of them stood in front of the open barn door, the crime scene tape grazing the underside of Bea's chin and the middle of Angela's chest. Angela stared at the empty center aisle of the barn, straining to remember the enchanting wedding setting that Fiona and Georgina had created there just days before. They'd brought it to life like magic, and it had disappeared just as fast.

"Just a plain old barn again."

"And murder scene, don't forget," Bea snickered. "That's a distinction few buildings enjoy."

"That ought to help with the marketing, if we ever decide to hold any weddings here," Angela said grimly. "It's every bride's dream: 'Have your wedding at the scene of a capital crime!'"

"You never know, girlie," Bea said. "Remember BettyCon? Who'd have thought so many people would love a Christmas-themed conference in

January? I bet people might love a murder-mystery themed vacation, too. Could be our next big thing."

"I think there are inns that offer mystery weekends," Angela said. "I'm guessing the murders aren't real, though. Call it a hunch."

"See?" Bea said. "We've got a leg up on the competition."

Angela took a few pictures of the barrel and the area around it with her phone, then lifted the tape a little bit. "Do you think we've got enough pictures, or were you thinking we'd sneak inside?" Angela kept her feet behind the tapeline, but stuck her head and shoulders under it and leaned forward to capture more of the crime scene area.

"Get some of the surrounding area, too. Lots of tire tracks."

"Those were from the rental companies. They wheeled the tables and chairs in on dollies, and must have wheeled them out that way, too," Angela said, snapping a few more pictures.

"Interesting," Bea said, scanning the area inquisitively. "Look over there." Bea pointed at the ground a couple of yards from where they were standing, close to the chicken coop. "Isn't that another chicken bone?"

"Yep," Angela said. She zoomed in and took another shot. "Seems weird. Are you thinking Rhonda was over here, snacking on wings, then someone killed her and dragged her into the barn?"

"Could be."

"It's pretty mean, even for Rhonda—eating chicken around chickens."

"Sounds just like Rhonda to me. No one escaped her wise-guy intimidation tactics, not even barnyard fowl. It's the poultry equivalent of a horse head on the pillow," Bea snickered, then looked down at the dirt. "No sign a body was dragged here, though."

"There's grass and dirt," Angela said. "Would you be able to tell if she was dragged?"

"Maybe, maybe not. I see partial footprints—but lots of people have walked here. Maybe someone offed Rhonda and carried her into the barn? Hard to imagine Georgina could do that. Rhonda was practically twice her size."

"Georgina could have lured her into the barn and done the deed inside. No carrying, no dragging. Here's a thought: Georgina texts Rhonda, tells her she wants to discuss something private. Rhonda comes to the barn, Georgina tells her she plans to team up with Fiona to do barn weddings.

Rhonda predictably shifts into bully mode. Georgina loses it, kills Rhonda with something she finds in that storage area. Or maybe it was more premeditated. Maybe she gets Rhonda to come to the barn and lies in wait behind the pipe and drape."

"That fits with Georgina telling everyone that Rhonda had left. So Georgina would have done this during the mixer—right before she told everyone Rhonda was gone."

"No one else said they got a text or any word from Rhonda that she was leaving early, right? Only Georgina. It has to be her, Bea. We've already caught her with the poison, don't forget. And I have to accept that George was a little too fond of hacking her way to success."

"I'm impressed that your mind's open to the dark side of your old friend, Angie, I really am," Bea said. "And the needleweed's another strike against her. But I have a feeling we're still missing some pieces. Georgina was hardly the only person who'd want to kill Rhonda. Might help if we'd seen more than Rhonda's dead foot. We don't have a clue how Rhonda died. Maybe McGregor will spill something about the coroner's report."

Angela nodded and snapped a few more pictures of the area near the barn, then they headed back to the inn.

~

"I've got good news and I've got better news. Which do you want first?" Bea said.

"Better start me off slow," said Pat's voice through the internet tube's speaker. "Good news first."

"Your strategy of avoiding greens saved you from the spewing sickness those unlucky mixer people got."

"You mean the food poisoning? The salad was the culprit?"

"I mean the *poison* poisoning. As in, it wasn't food poisoning, because a real-life poisoner was the culprit. And we're pretty sure the salad was the vehicle. Angela found a poisonous plant called needleweed in the kitchen."

"Fascinating. I'll stick with my meat-potatoes-salt-sugar eating program for now. So what's the better news?"

"I've got a gig for you today, if you're free. Easy money. Helping out the local police. McGregor's not paying your regular rate, but I'll make up the difference. You'll be guarding a crime scene here at the inn."

"I can be up there in about an hour. But did you say 'crime scene'? Does this mean you've got bad news, too?"

"Oopsie, forgot that part. My bad. We've had another suspicious death here at the inn—that part's not so good. But the victim was Rhonda, so…."

"No shortage of suspects."

"And no surplus of tears. By the way, I was planning to call you today to ask you about the night of the mixer, when you followed Rhonda up to park at Heavenly West."

"What about it?"

"Where did she park? She didn't put her car in Connie's half-built house, did she?"

Pat laughed. "Why would she do that? She parked in the lot like everyone else."

"That's what I figured. But her car somehow ended up inside Connie's shell of a garage, with a tarp over it."

"Someone moved it, then. But who?"

"My thoughts exactly. Or more precisely, who moved it, when did they move it, and why?"

"I've got a lot more questions than those three, Bea."

"Don't you worry. There'll be plenty of time for me to fill you in on the whole story when you get up here."

~

LEXIE WAS ALMOST TO SACRAMENTO WHEN HER cell phone rang. With the help of the time difference, she'd already had a quick crack-of-dawn chat with her freelancer friend in Florida. As luck would have it, he'd worked on that wedding fair story a while, before the trail went cold and he'd gotten on the tail of something hotter. He promised to dig up some files later and send them Lexie's way.

In the meantime, Lexie decided not to waste any time in talking to Dennis Poundstone, and maybe Sandy Givens, too. She thought she could kill a couple birds with one stone, maybe more, with one quick trip to Sacramento. She knew she'd be tapped to work on the Rhonda murder story, so why not get background on that while nosing around about the wedding fair scam and related dirt? This way, the *Grapevine* would help fund her little side investigation, and she wouldn't have to sell the idea to her cheapskate publisher.

Once the exposé was written, she felt confident it would sell itself.

She was driving and smiling, visions of journalism prizes and career glory swimming in her head, when the call interrupted her intoxicating daydream.

She didn't recognize the number. "Lexie Greene," she said into the speaker.

"It's Angela Garcia."

"Angela. What can I do for you?"

Lexie managed to act casual, even though she knew why Angela was calling. Angela had every reason to be distressed about that article, but Lexie couldn't do a thing about it. Her boss truly believed in the old newspaper trope that if it bleeds, it leads, and the inn's misfortune was likely to generate a lot of clicks. Lexie wouldn't be so foolish as to waste what little political capital she had complaining about it. As the lowest person on the ladder at *Wine Country Grapevine,* Lexie was constantly on the verge of being let go. Best she could do was try to smooth Angela over and hope the story died down fast.

"I'm sure you've guessed why I'm calling—that article," Angela said. Lexie felt her heartbeat tick up a notch. She took a deep breath to slow it down.

"Listen," Angela said, "I know you're going to tell me you didn't write it—"

"Correct."

"—and you probably can't do anything about it."

"Also correct."

"OK, but didn't you tell me that keeping one of the *Grapevine's* biggest advertisers happy was a priority?"

"Yes. If you're threatening to pull your ads, though, you should probably talk to the publisher."

"Nothing like that yet. But I'd like a chance to respond to that story. You already know—and I thank you for telling me—that the 'poisoning' was probably sabotage by one of the vendors at the mixer. And guess what? I think we've figured out how it was done, and even who probably did it. I'd just like to write some kind of rebuttal—or even better, maybe you could write a story looking at this angle. Is that something you can help with?"

Lexie found herself grinning—and feeling happy that she wasn't on a video call. Definitive evidence of a wedding vendor poisoning colleagues would be a perfect vignette for her side project with Bea! *Speaking of which*, Lexie wondered, *does Angela even know about that?* Lexie didn't know her well, but she knew Angela could be more than a little jealous. Best to test the waters.

"I'd love to discuss it with you, Angela. I'm actually on my way to Sacramento—"

"Sacramento? Why?"

Glad I checked. I guess she doesn't know. Hmm... how much to tell her?

"I'm going to see Sandy Givens. I guess I don't need to tell you that our barn wedding story is probably killed—at least for the time being—thanks to Rhonda also, you know, being killed."

Lexie was embroidering on the fly, and having fun with it.

"I figured you might have heard."

"Word gets around. Anyway, I thought it would be kinder to tell Sandy about our story's fate in person."

"Kind of a long drive, though, no? Don't stories get killed all the time?"

"You're right," Lexie said, her voice still cool as ice water. "But not usually because of a colleague's murder. If she hasn't heard about it yet, it would be kind of jarring to hear it over the phone. I also thought she and I might brainstorm another use for the images—maybe the *Grapevine* would allow a Sacramento-area publication to use my copy, once interest in Rhonda's murder died down.

"Plus, you know, Angela, I might as well be up front and tell you I'm almost certainly going to be covering Rhonda's murder. Crime beat, anything requiring a lot of legwork—you know that all rolls down to me. So I thought I could start learning more about the victim today, too."

"I figured you'd be on the story. But I hope you won't be too surprised when I bar you from the crime scene."

"Nope. I've got a job to do, and so do you. At least you can't lock me out of Sacramento."

"Thanks for understanding."

"There's hope for our friendship yet, wouldn't you say?" Lexie waited for Angela to respond, but instead there was an awkward silence. "About that response to the food poisoning story you're hoping for, who do you like for the poisoner? It's gotta be Georgina, or maybe Georgina doing it for Rhonda, right?"

"Georgina. But how'd you guess?"

"Process of elimination. Only Fiona, Sandy, and Georgina had my personal email. One of them had to be the anonymous source that tipped me off about the poisoning at your inn. Sandy was in the hospital, and Fiona—"

"Yeah. Fiona doesn't seem like the type. Listen, you might as well know, Bea and I caught Georgina covering her poison tracks. I'm pretty sure she's not just our poisoner, but the murderer—and the police think so, too."

"I guess that makes my job easier. Open and shut. My murder story could make a perfect rebuttal to the food-borne illness article," Lexie said. "Listen, Angela, I'm going to hang up—lots of traffic ahead—but before I go, I'm sorry about Georgina. I know she was your friend."

Angela was quiet for a moment.

"Angela?"

"Sorry. It's… it's starting to sink in. Weird feeling, knowing you've been best friends with a murderer."

~

"Angela, I've got an update," Sergeant McGregor said. "Officer Carroll got a late start, and it looks like he'll hit some Tahoe traffic on the way back with the suspect. We won't get back to your place until tomorrow."

Angela stood up from her desk and stretched, switching her cellphone to speaker mode with a tap. "OK. But what about the crime scene? Pat's already been out there guarding it for several hours."

"Do the best you can. Can you persuade Pat to do an overnight? I don't suppose you could get your techie boyfriend to set up some kind of camera?"

"I'll see what I can figure out."

"Thanks. And one more thing, Angela. Georgina Peterson keeps asking for you to come by the station once we get her booked. Said she doesn't even want to talk to a lawyer—just you."

Angela didn't respond, unsure what to say.

"You don't have to do it if you don't want to," McGregor said. "I'll be there, if it helps. You could bring Miss Sickles, too."

Angela sighed. "Text me when you're ready for me."

Angela shut the door behind her and headed out to the barn. Pat and Bea were sitting beyond the police tape in folding chairs. Aseem was standing beside them.

"Hi Angel," Aseem said, smiling hopefully. Angela ignored him and focused on Bea and Pat.

"I got some news from McGregor. He won't be coming by this afternoon—or at all, until tomorrow morning. Pat, any chance you can pull an overnighter? Maybe Bea and I can take over for a few hours later this afternoon. You could grab a nap in one of the empty suites."

Pat looked dubious and began to hem and haw.

"I'll do it," Aseem said. "I don't mind. You know I like staying up late. I could take over after dinner —say, eight o'clock?"

"Sounds like a perfect solution," Bea said.

"On second thought, I don't know why Mc-Gregor's so worried about watching the crime scene anyway. They're bringing Georgina in as we speak. With the killer in custody, who's going to disrupt the scene?" Angela squinted and cupped her chin in her hand. "There's only one person I can think of: Aseem's old girlfriend. I'm sure our intrepid reporter will want to nose around the crime scene, but instead of keeping her out, Aseem, you'd probably just show her around. Thank you, but I'll pass on your offer." Then she shot a smirk in Aseem's direction and turned on her heel and walked away.

"You know Lexie was never my girlfriend!" Aseem yelled uselessly at her back. Then he turned to Bea and Pat and tried to lighten the mood. "Think she's still mad at me?"

"Don't worry, handsome," Bea said. "She'll come around."

"I want to help. I think I should set up a

stakeout tonight and watch the crime scene. What if Georgina had an accomplice? That person might try to tamper with evidence."

"Good idea. Besides, what if Georgina didn't do it?"

"Do you think that's possible? It would be much better for Angel, right?"

"You mean if her old friend was not a murderer?" Bea cackled. "Methinks so."

"Maybe Georgina wasn't even the poisoner. When I left Gary's—I mean, you know, Fiona's—I went to see Paige, the caterer. I couldn't help thinking that the caterer would have the most opportunity to poison the food—or, at least, she'd know who else had that opportunity."

"Sounds like a longshot," Bea said. "Wouldn't that damage her own reputation? She might even destroy her own business."

"That's what Fiona said, but I couldn't let go of the idea. Then it occurred to me that the poisoning might not be about sabotaging the inn, or targeting anyone personally—what if someone wanted to sabotage Paige's business and the inn was collateral damage? So I went to see Paige, and she told me a few things. She said some of the other vendors had access to the kitchen. Georgina and Rhonda, of course

—they were in the kitchen a lot. Wedding planners have access to everything during an event, to keep on top of the timing, and might even help occasionally with small things, if the caterers get too busy."

"We've been assuming Georgina and Rhonda had access to the kitchen—that's why they're suspects."

"There's more. Paige said that vendors who won't get a chance to eat during the event can leave stuff in the walk-in, and she often leaves snacks for them to have after the event. That expands the pool of possible poisoners. At least the DJs, who were performing for most of the mixer, and others vendors doing jobs for the event, could be on the list. They were all permitted to go in the kitchen at their convenience.

"But here's the kicker: when I asked Paige if someone in the group could have sabotaged her, she said, and I quote, 'Who would dare?!'"

"'Who would dare?' She sounds like she's taken Rhonda lessons!" Bea cackled.

"Funny you should say that. The full thing she said was, 'Who would dare?! I'm paying Rhonda's protection money. It stinks, and none of us like it —but at least everyone knows not to mess with any of us. Look what happened to Dennis when he crossed her—Rhonda made an example of him.'"

"Does this mean she could still be Rhonda's killer, even if she wasn't the saboteur? They don't have to be the same person, do they?" Pat asked.

"Seems to me that she thought she had a good thing going. Giving in to mobsters hurts, but once you do, why give up the benefits?" Bea said.

"That puts the spotlight on people outside Rhonda's gang," Pat said.

"Where does that leave us?" Bea said.

"I'm not sure," Aseem said. "But there was one more little mystery I asked Paige about: the desserts. Why didn't she serve them?"

"Lemme guess," Bea said. "Rhonda told her not to. Or someone told her that Rhonda said not to."

"Exactly. She showed me a text Rhonda sent her, telling her not to serve dessert. The text definitely came from Rhonda's cell. Paige had left a batch of cream in the big mixer in the kitchen, ready to whip. Paige and her assistant were busy serving, and it was a simple task, so Paige asked Rhonda to help. Rhonda said she'd turn the mixer on, then turn it off when it was done. Shouldn't have taken more than five or ten minutes with that big mixer."

"Rhonda's text said there was a problem with the whipped cream."

"How'd you guess?

"Just a hunch. I wish we knew for sure how Rhonda died. I never thought I'd say this even once, but for the second time today, I really wish Sergeant Lazybones would enlighten us."

CHAPTER 15

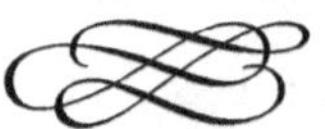

*L*exie left Sandy Givens' house hungry for details. The more she learned about the conniving behavior of certain figures in the local wedding scene, the more she knew she was onto a real story. She was keen—almost desperate!—to get to the meat of it.

Lexie took a breath and reminded herself what her mother used to say to her when she got impatient as a little girl:

Patience, hummingbird.

Lexie knew that sometimes it takes a while to get the full story. You have to put the time in. You have to pull on threads. And you have to gently push. Sometimes it's hard to get people on the record at first.

Especially when they're afraid.

Sandy Givens had been afraid.

Sandy had tried to shrug it off, but Lexie clearly saw the fear below the surface. Lexie had felt her blood pumping as she recognized it.

What was that idea an old mentor instilled in her about chasing a story? Make haste slowly. Proceed with urgency, but don't rush critical steps. Be sure not to miss anything important.

"If you want to know why Dennis brought up that wedding fair scandal out of Chicago," Sandy had said, "you should ask him. If he remembers, he'll tell you. He's not one to mince words. Why would he bother at this point?"

Sandy looked guilty as she said it, though it was nothing more than the truth. Because by tangling with Rhonda, Dennis had shot his own business in the foot.

Or maybe, as it turned out, in the head. Sandy even confided that it seemed like Dennis hadn't just given up on his big dreams of owning a downtown ballroom, he might be on the verge of packing it in altogether.

That was when I was sure Sandy was afraid. Sandy had done the math: one careless confrontation with Rhonda might have cost Dennis everything.

And now, talking to Dennis himself, Lexie felt sure that Sandy had been right about all of it.

Dennis said he didn't know why he'd blurted the idea that Rhonda's wedding fair could be a scam, like the one he'd heard about from the DJs.

"It was just on my mind. My guys had just come back from the annual DJ conference in Las Vegas, and they were buzzing about the scandal. The whole conference was buzzing about it. See, mobile DJs spend a lot on wedding advertising. A wedding fair scam was bound to get their attention.

"Funny thing, though," Dennis added wryly, "Rhonda's reaction didn't convince me I'd been wrong to ask the question. She never tried selling a wedding fair again after that, even though she'd been so excited about it.

"I can't help imagining she might have planned to scam us and go on the run, like whoever did that fake fair in Chicago. I know it's far-fetched. More likely, she started having too much fun bossing our industry around. Maybe she decided she liked it here in Cowtown. Who knows? But it makes me laugh to think about the possibility. Gotta have a laugh or two in this crazy life, right?"

Lexie smiled. "Won't be any crying from your

crew when they hear the news that she's dead, I guess."

"Oh, I'm sure they know already. I got the call from Sandy a little while ago, and I doubt I was first on her list. Gossip spreads like wildfire in wedding world—and this bit's juicier than most."

Sheesh. Sandy must have started spreading the news the second I left her house.

"Rhonda will hardly be missed by anyone. Except maybe her little gang, but that's just because they'll be on their own now. Unless, I suppose… unless someone is in the wings, hoping to take over her racket. We wedding pros don't make that much, but that percentage off every gig adds up. Probably adds up even more when you're on the receiving end of it."

"Huh. So are you thinking someone in her protection circle could have a motive to kill her—to take over? That adds to the list of suspects."

"How should I know? I'm just glad I can't be called a suspect. Almost makes me glad I spent a night and a day puking my guts up."

"Dennis, did anyone ever tell you you've got a way with words?"

As Lexie mulled what Dennis had said—in particular, his offhand speculation that someone "in the wings" could take over Rhonda's racket—

she considered the overlap of her two stories. She'd driven up to Sacramento to explore the possibility of hidden corruption in the local wedding community, planning to ask the same sources a few questions about Rhonda's death for her crime beat story, to ensure that the *Grapevine* would pay her per diem. Now she had the feeling the two stories were much more related than she'd assumed.

And here I was thinking someone killed Rhonda simply because they hated her.

"Dennis, since I drove all the way up here, do you think I could talk to one of your DJs today?"

"It's a Sunday in May," he said, laughing. "Judging by your outfit, you either forgot it was Sunday or you're not much of a religious type."

Lexie looked down at the tight-fitting tank top she was wearing, and the navel ring and tattoo it left exposed. "Whatever do you mean?" Lexie said. "Yeah, I forgot it was Sunday. Every day's a day for a journalist. But…what's your point?"

"The DJ—I'm down to one now, and he's working today. Sundays in May are usually booked with weddings. You might want to talk to my limo driver, though," Dennis had said. "Maybe he remembers something."

"Limo driver?"

"He's driving now, but he was DJing for me back then. He's got a brunch wedding today, and afterwards he'll be back at HQ for a few hours before the next gig."

Lexie pulled into an industrial park full of warehouses with office suites attached. At the end of the long aisle of huge garage doors and branded office entrances, Lexie spotted the sign for Destination Dream's "HQ." DJ Tad's van, with "Get Granny Dancing" plastered all over it, was parked near the office door.

That's unfortunate, Lexie thought, wondering if she should watch for Tad to leave before heading inside. Would she get anything out of the driver about the wedding fair scam if Tad, one of Rhonda's circle, was in the room? The driver would probably clam up. Lexie decided to wait.

But what if they're talking about Rhonda?

Lexie found a space a few doors past Destination Dream and walked back toward the office. Before going inside, she peeked carefully around the side of the open warehouse door, hoping to avoid being seen. Tad was there, talking animatedly with the limo driver. They were both wearing tuxedos—Tad must have come from a wedding, like the driver. Or maybe he was on his way to one.

Lexie stepped inside the office, hoping to eavesdrop. And she got lucky: at the end of the long, narrow waiting area was a door to the warehouse, and it was half-open. She scooted past the opening and stood in the corner, looking through the space near the hinges. The gap was so slender, she couldn't make out much of what was going on in the warehouse. The two men mostly kept their backs turned toward her. *Drat.* She put her ear to the crack and strained to hear bits of the conversation.

"Ready? Count it out in front of me, would ya?" Tad said.

Count what?

"I know it's all there," the driver said, after counting to thirty.

"Gotta love brides who give cash tips," Tad laughed.

Thirty tens? Thirty hundreds? If it was thirty hundreds... three thousand bucks is a lot of cash. Who's paying whom?

"And the other thing," the driver said.

"Yes," Tad said.

"What's with the glove? Got a Michael Jackson theme at your next wedding?"

"At the Oro Lindo? Not quite classy enough for that place," Tad laughed. "Nah—" Lexie missed a few words—"gave me a rash"—Tad spoke too softly again—"gross out the guests."

More words that Lexie couldn't hear... then "take care of the other thing."

Lexie heard the driver say sure, and thought she heard jangling keys. She squinted through the crack again, frustrated that the two men had stepped farther from the door.

"Pleasure doing business with you," the driver said. "I heard about Rhonda. Is it too much to hope things will go back to how they were?"

Still straining to see, Lexie thought she saw a set of shoulders shrug.

"Not sure I know what you mean by 'how things were.' Rhonda and I got to town around the same time. Listen, I've got a wedding—"

"Of course. Like I said—"

"Pleasure's all mine. Hey, are those things wrapped with your Destination Dream logos candy bars?"

"Yeah, promotional items. Dennis likes them. He says chocolate puts everyone in a good mood, and people in a good mood are more likely to book."

"Interesting. Could you spare one? I'm hungry, and I don't have much time before I have to get to the next gig. And, you know, who doesn't love chocolate?"

"Sure. I'd take that white glove off before eating it, though. Chocolate stains on a white glove—not classy."

"Ha—good point, dude. How about one more? Could you drop it into my pocket?"

Through the crack, Lexie saw Tad was heading out of the warehouse door. She hustled to the front of the office to look through the tinted glass, standing to the side to be sure she couldn't be seen. Tad walked down two doors to a trash can. He opened the bar he was holding carefully with his thumb, using only his gloved hand, then shook the chocolate out into the can and carried the wrapper back to his car.

Lexie looked indecisively at the door to the warehouse, then back at Tad's van. Maybe she should have followed Tad, but she gambled that he was heading right to his next gig. If she was right, he'd be at Oro Lindo for hours. She could start tailing him there later, and not miss anything important in between.

"Hi, my name's Lexie," she said as she walked through the office door to the warehouse. "Dennis said I could find you here."

THE WAIT FOR MCGREGOR'S CALL SEEMED LIKE AN eternity. Angela tried to pass the time by catching up on email and social media messages, but, since she rarely fell behind, that kept her attention for less than half an hour. Before long, she'd even gotten her least favorite tasks, like budgeting, well in hand. Reluctantly, she decided to reorganize her closet.

Anything to stop obsessing about what she was going to say to Georgina.

The sun was setting by the time she put the last pair of shoes in its place in her new wardrobe configuration (by season—previously, she'd organized everything by color). She walked over to her nightstand and turned on the light. The clock, embedded in a charming, cheery sculpture of a snowy Christmas scene, said it was already after eight.

Surely McGregor—or, as Bea would say, "Sergeant Lazybones"—wasn't working this late.

Angela chuckled to herself and decided she should plan on heading to the police station in the morning. The sound of her phone startled her.

"Sorry for the late call, Angela," McGregor said. "Like I said, Tahoe traffic was bad, and it took longer to deal with our partners up in Sac. We just got done with Georgina Peterson's paperwork, if you want to head on over. You can wait until the tomorrow if you prefer, but it would have to be in the afternoon, since Officer Carroll and I will be coming over your way to examine the scene in the morning. Miss Peterson is really hoping to see you as soon as you can. I won't lie, she's rather upset."

"Being arrested for murder probably does that to a person. I'll be over soon."

Angela found Bea and they drove in silence past long rows of vines and wineries to the little police station on Main. Angela pulled into the lot and parked in one of the three spaces.

"Ready?"

"No. What do I say to her?"

"You don't have to say anything, Angie. See what she has to say first."

Angela nodded and the two of them made their way into the station. McGregor was waiting for them just inside the door.

"Nice of you to stay late for us, Sarge," Bea said, making an effort to be respectful.

McGregor eyed her through a squint and tilted his head. "It's a murder case, Sickles. Still a very big deal around here—despite your inn's additions to our body count."

"What can I say? Betty Snickerdoodle's popular with all sorts of people!" Bea cackled.

"Angela, are you ready? You can go in to see the suspect. You know the way—it's Beatrice's old cell."

Bea frowned. "Don't say it so proudly, Beef Jerky. Yet another time you captured the wrong person!"

"I thought you knew better than to call me that, Tater Tot."

"Hey, you two!" Angela cried, throwing up her hands. "What happened to your truce? And your commitment to professionalism?"

"Sorry, Angie," Bea said. "Sorry, Sergeant Laz—I mean, sorry, Sergeant McGregor."

"Me, too," McGregor said. Bea held her small fist up for a bump against McGregor's burly one.

"Bea, you're coming in with me, right? I don't want to go alone."

Angela and Bea walked through the door in the rear of the station office into the holding cell area. Bea shuddered under the archway. "Can't say I'm thrilled to be back here."

Georgina was sitting on the little bench in the

cell. Her eyes were red from crying, and her beautiful complexion was blotchy and puffy and still damp with tears. She wasn't wearing gloves, though her hands were still covered with the angry red rash.

"Thank you for coming, Angela," she said, rushing to the front of the cell.

Angela nodded.

"I know I haven't been the greatest friend. OK, I'm a terrible friend." Georgina paused and looked down. Angela didn't respond.

"What I'm going to tell you is going to make you hate me forever, even though I'm so, so sorry. But before I tell you, there's something else you must know. And I beg you to believe me."

Georgina tilted her head back up and stared straight into Angela's eyes with a beseeching look full of guilt and pain.

Angela's expression was unchanged. "Spit it out, Georgina." Bea looked at Angela and smiled faintly, resting her hand gently at Angela's elbow.

"The thing you must know is," Georgina said, starting to cry again. "I didn't kill Rhonda."

"Why would I believe you? You certainly had a motive. You hated her, right?" Angela said dispassionately. "And I see your 'poison ivy' hasn't cleared up."

"I'm not sad that she's dead. But I could never

kill her—or anyone. Angela, you know me, don't you? I haven't changed like that. You know I could never… yes, I've done bad things. But I could never go that far."

"Well, at least you're admitting that you're not above cheating or scamming to get what you want."

"I know why you think that. But promise me you'll try to believe me. I didn't kill Rhonda." Georgina sucked in a huge breath. "I didn't kill Rhonda… but… I know you know this already… the poison in the salad… that was me." Tears were streaming down Georgina's face. "I had a friend pose as the inspector—"

"We never would have guessed he was fake," Bea snarked.

"—and I took the battery out of your alarm. I did all that. I admit it—but I didn't kill Rhonda."

"Why can't you grow up, Georgina? Your slippery tricks were sort of entertaining in college, but aren't you ever going to act like an adult? Build a reputation for doing what you promise?"

Georgina started to whimper again. "I have been, Angela. I swear. I am—was—good at my job. I worked hard at it. A lot of brides liked my work —it's true, really. And I was being patient, waiting my turn, even when Rhonda broke all her promises."

"Taste of your own medicine is usually bitter. Why should I believe you? You had every motive to kill Rhonda. You could have been planning to take over her business. You just admitted you have a track record of shady shortcuts. You just admitted to poisoning your own colleagues!"

"You saw me doing the announcements at the mixer. I wasn't prepared. I had no idea where Rhonda went—and I still don't. I'd just been taking a little break, walking the grounds of the inn, when I got her text, and next thing you know, Tad's texting me too, telling me to get ready to do the announcements. And when I got up on stage, I could tell people were getting ill from the needle-weed, and I started to panic."

Angela and Bea looked at each other.

"You did look nervous," Bea said. "But if you weren't expecting people to get sick from the salads, why'd you poison them in the first place?"

"I just… I guess I just snapped. Seeing you, Angela, and hearing about all your success with the inn and your publishing. Perfect Angela, top of the class again, just like always. Everything's easy for you."

"Easy? Easy?" Angela shouted. "Do you have

any idea how much hard work I've put into these things?"

"Hard work comes easy to you!"

Bea couldn't suppress a chuckle. "She has a point, Angie."

"Bea! She could have killed someone with that needleweed. In fact, Georgina—we still don't know if one of the guests made it out of the hospital alive!"

"I was sure it wouldn't kill anybody—at least, I didn't think so. I told you, I'm not a murderer. I know I messed up."

"You made people dangerously ill, Georgina. Not to mention the cost—the ambulances, the hospital. Poor Dennis—it probably cost him thousands of dollars, and you and Rhonda and everyone else in her gang have already crippled his business as it is."

Georgina bowed her head and lowered her voice. "Of course you're right, Angela. And I am prepared to be punished for what I did. Please, you must believe me, though. I didn't kill Rhonda. Maybe you don't want to believe it for my sake, but shouldn't Rhonda's real killer be punished, too?"

Georgina backed away from the cell bars and sat down on the bench, face in hands, crying.

"Please at least believe me that I'm not a murderer. I'm not a murderer."

Angela and Bea were quiet for an awkward moment. Angela finally said, "You do realize that if that guest dies, you'll be charged for that, don't you? You should get yourself a lawyer, Georgina. I'll think about the rest of it."

"Thank you. And I know I have no right to ask, Angela, but could you do one favor for me? Could you call Tad and tell him I don't need his help? I just need to figure this out on my own. Tell him not to try to contact me. I'm going to own up to what I did, I promise you. Hearing from Tad will only make it harder."

Angela nodded and walked out of the station, not realizing Bea stayed behind.

"You and Tad—are you two a couple?" Bea asked.

"No," Georgina said. "Why do people always ask that?"

"Why do you think they ask?"

"He's always hovering, trying to help me. I like him, and I know he means well, but… please don't make me say it."

"He's not good enough for you, toots? Is that the problem?"

"It's not like that… it's… Haven't I owned up to

enough flaws for one night?" Georgina said through a piteous sigh.

"Girl like you's bound to get advances galore," Bea said. "You don't have to accept a single one of them if you don't want to. Since you're on a self-improvement kick, though, you might want to add not using men and leading them on to your list of resolutions."

Georgina didn't respond, just continued to weep softly.

Bea walked past the desks in the front of the station, held a finger up to McGregor, and leaned out the door. "Give me a minute, Angie. I want to ask McGregor something."

"Did you hear all that back there, McGregor?" Bea said. "Would it surprise you if I told you I think it's all true? I don't like Georgina for the murder."

McGregor rolled his eyes dubiously. "Really, Jessica Fletcher? What makes you so sure?"

"I'm feeling generous. I'll be happy to share a few things I've figured out," Bea said. "But first, how about you tell me how ol' Rhonda met her maker?"

"You first."

"OK, here's one thing I know for sure. Rhonda didn't die in that barn. I bet she was killed hours before she ended up under that wine barrel."

"And how do you know that, Sickles?"

"Your turn now, Sarge."

"Coroner hasn't done a complete investigation, but it looks like Rhonda's neck was broken. In several places."

"I thought so. I'd say that makes it even less likely that little Georgina pulled it off, wouldn't you? Did the coroner happen to mention if Rhonda had whipped cream on her?"

"No," McGregor laughed. "But he did say she had some sticky stuff on her that he hadn't identified yet."

"When you tell him it's whipped cream, also tell him I said 'you're welcome.'"

Bea turned back to the door and reached for the handle.

"And one other thing, Sarge. I've been thinking this killer probably didn't off Rhonda all by their lonesome. Now I'm almost sure of it."

CHAPTER 16

Bea and Angela said little on the way back to the inn. Bea tried in the gentlest way she could muster to get Angela to talk. But all Angela had to say was, "I don't know what to think, Bea. I suppose it would be a relief to know for sure my friend wasn't a murderer. She admits she poisoned people because she was jealous of me, though." Then it was Bea's turn to be silent.

They turned the corner into the inn's driveway, and Angela spotted a car in the distance, near the barn. She stopped to look more closely, trying to discern whose it was in the dark.

"That's not Pat's car—that looks like Aseem's," she frowned. "I told him not to—never mind." Angela sighed and drove forward to park.

"You know, Aseem's just trying to show you he cares," Bea said as they walked into the inn. "And if Georgina's not the killer, don't you think it might be a good thing Aseem's keeping watch over the crime scene, in case the real killer is thinking about tampering with evidence?"

"Maybe you're right. He should have asked Pat for stake-out lessons, though. He's not exactly in-conspicuous with his laptop glowing in the dark."

"He's there to deter people, not catch them, girlie."

"He's probably already working on apps for his new boss. A crook could walk right by and Aseem probably wouldn't notice.

"You should talk to him, girlie. Let him tell his side of the story."

"Maybe tomorrow. It's been another long day, and McGregor will be here in the morning."

BACK IN HER SUITE, BEA SAW THE RING ON THE TOP of her internet speaker glowing. "Rebecca, play my messages."

"One new message," Rebecca announced. "Bea, it's Lexie. I've had quite a day, and it's not over yet." Lexie recounted the highlights of her conversations with Sandy, Dennis, and the limo driver, plus the exchange she'd overheard between him and Tad.

"I'm tailing Tad. At the moment, I'm just waiting. You know what's more boring than waiting for a wedding reception to end? Waiting in a car for a wedding reception you're not even attending to end. I'm going to turn my phone off—it's bright, and I'm trying not to be noticed. I'll call if trailing Tad turns up anything interesting. I'm just following a hunch, but I won't be surprised if I wind up following him to his house after all this. That would be a big waste of time, but we'll see.

"Oh, and some interesting news from my free-lancer friend about the wedding fair scam story in Chicago. He sent me a bunch of links and notes. One detail caught my eye. Seems they had a sales rep that no one had met—everything was done over email—and people just knew him as 'George.' Caught my attention, at first because it just seemed odd that it would be a guy," she added with a laugh. "Call me sexist, but it's hard to picture a guy selling space in a bridal fair. Then I saw one of my friend's notes had a full name, and it hit me: I'd heard that name before. Anyone who's taken feminist literature would know it—"

Lexie's voice almost seemed to disappear, she

started whispering so quietly. "Shoot, gotta go. People are coming out. Bye!"

"Thanks for confirming another of my suspicions, cub reporter. Just a few more missing pieces to fit," Bea said aloud. She pulled her cane out of her closet and began marching around the room. "Never too early to start envisioning my big reveal! But how will I get everyone in the same room this time?"

ANGELA REACHED HER SUITE AND BELLY-FLOPPED onto her bed, her face planted in her pillow. Processing everything Georgina had said was overwhelming. Could she dare to believe her "old friend"? Or was her hopeful nature getting the better of her again?

She rolled over onto her side and looked at the clock. Nearly eleven. Too late to call her mother for her opinion. Out of habit, she thought about asking Aseem for advice.

Should I just walk right out to his car and ask him what he thinks? Pick up where we left off?

She had to admit she wanted to.

Oh, right. Maybe I'll interrupt him working on his fancy new job.

The image of Aseem tapping on his laptop annoyed her—but also gave her an idea.

She rolled off the bed, sat down at her desk, and began searching the web on her laptop.

"Georgina Peterson wedding planner" turned up almost nothing: just Georgina's listing on a career network and her bland bio on Rhonda's Marry Well business site—.

Let's see how people like Marry Well.

Angela searched for reviews and found hundreds for Rhonda's company.

Three-star average. How... average. Angela chuckled to herself.

The average didn't tell the real story. Most of the reviews were two stars, with a few furious one-star comments. The average was propped up by a group of five-star reviews, all posted around the same time. Angela clicked on some of them and found fakes so obvious, they made her laugh out loud.

```
        "Rhonda is a wedding planning
                genius!!!!"
       "Rhonda saved my wedding!!!!"
         "Don't use Rhonda as your
      wedding planner unless you want
       a unique, fabulous, affordable
```

<pre>
wedding that will be the envy
    of all your friends!!!!"
"Rhonda is simply the best!!!!"
"Don't take risks with your big
   day. Marry Well and hire
      Rhonda!!!!"
</pre>

You'd think she'd have been smart enough to change up the number of exclamation points.

Angela clicked through the bad reviews. They looked much more authentic and mostly shared the same unhappy themes: Rhonda was rude. Rhonda bullied brides into hiring her "preferred" vendors. Rhonda overcharged. Rhonda was no fun to be around—which ironically, she rarely seemed to be when you needed her.

But another theme kept popping up in many of the critical posts.

"Thank heavens for Georgina. Without her help, I would have gone crazy."

"Rhonda was horrible, but Georgina was always there for us."

"Georgina worked so hard. Poor thing. She almost made up for her horrible boss."

"If Georgina started her own wedding planning business, I'd recommend it. Georgina, if you're reading this, do it!"

Embedded in the midst of bitter complaints, the praise for Georgina looked genuine. And Angela knew from her own experience that for every sincere positive remark, there might be a dozen other people who felt the same but didn't write reviews. It seemed like maybe, just maybe, Georgina had been telling the truth about trying to change her ways.

Angela pushed back from her desk and sighed.

Why does everything have to be so complicated?

Hoping Connie might still be awake, Angela stood by the connecting door and knocked quietly.

"Connie, you awake?" she whispered. She knocked again, a little more forcefully, and asked the question again, a little louder.

"Sure, honey, c'mon in," Connie said, releasing her hand from the switch on her bedside lamp just as Angela made it over the threshold. She scooted upright on the bed, leaning against the headboard, and patted on the empty side. "Sit down and tell me what's going on."

"I'm sorry. I know I woke you up. I'm just… it's been another strange day." She told Connie about what Georgina had said—how she'd confessed to the poisoning even as she tried to convince Angela she was changing for the better.

"Why do people have to be so confusing?" Angela fretted. "Sometimes it seems like you can't trust your own mind."

"I think I get what this is really about. Honey, you need to talk to him," Connie said. "People can be complicated, of course I agree with that. And you know I'm no great expert at relationships, may Billy Ray Bandy rest in peace," she added, looking up at the ceiling. "It's because of my own failures that I've hesitated to offer an opinion, but now it's clear that I must. *Anyone* can see how you and Aseem feel for each other. *Especially* how he feels for you. You simply *must* give the poor man a chance to explain!"

"I think you're right," Angela said.

"I am! And he'll be sitting outside all night with nothing to do. What better time than the present?"

"Thank you, Connie."

Angela got up from the bed and reached down to pet Bijou, who was at her feet. "Bijou, how about a walk?"

She snapped a leash on the dog and walked through her suite out to the hall, grabbing a hoodie along the way. They walked out through the dark, quiet reception area. The night air was crisp and the sky was clear and scattered with stars.

As they made their way toward the barn, Bijou stopped to sniff at inexplicably alluring scents and objects along the side of the path. As they approached Aseem's car, Angela noticed the light on the driver's side door was on. The door was slightly open, and must have been that way long enough for the overhead light to time out.

They got to the car and Angela opened the door: no Aseem. His laptop appeared to have been hastily tossed onto the passenger seat, and was resting precariously on the narrow edge of its screen. As she set it upright on its base, Angela couldn't help noticing what Aseem had been working on: an email to her.

She gasped as she read its first line, and then the next.

"I had to put my thoughts in writing, Angel, and not just because we're not talking to each other right now. I want to be sure I get things right this time. I'm sorry, Angel. You're right. I did lie to you."

Bijou intruded on Angela's thoughts by tugging at the leash.

Am I wrong to keep reading this?

But she'd already read the next paragraph… and the next.

"Not about the job. I wasn't looking for a job, I

promise you. Gary said he might want to invest in those apps I've been coding on the side, and I knew, at least I thought I knew, that it wouldn't amount to anything. Who meets Gary Wheaton at a wedding mixer and winds up getting an investment? It just seemed like a pipe dream. And I honestly thought I'd be meeting with one of his employees. Someone more like a peer. I rationalized that saying I'd be meeting with a 'tech dude buddy' wasn't that far off from reality.

"The truth is, I didn't want to build up my hopes, and I didn't want you to be disappointed in me. I figured I'd tell you all about it after, when it was all over, and we'd have a laugh about my brief moment in the sun of Gary Wheaton.

"I see now I did the wrong thing. I'm so proud of you, Angel, and I guess I just wanted you to be proud of me, too."

Angela felt so touched, tears began to well in her eyes. But it was the next sentence that made them fall.

"You see, Angel, I'm still learning what to do, because I've never been in love before."

"Oh Bijou, I've had it all wrong. We've got to find him. Where could he have gone?" Angela leaned down and looked in the dachshund's eyes and said, "Where's Aseem, girl?" wondering if the dog had a clue what she meant. "Let's go find him."

Angela closed Aseem's laptop and tucked it under her arm, shut the car door, and jogged to the front entrance of the inn, Bijou running happily beside her. Her mind was racing with thoughts that were alternately giddy and guilty, and with desperation to get to Aseem's suite and find him. When they reached the reception area, instead of following her down the hall, Bijou tugged the leash in the direction of the small hallway that led to the kitchen.

"Really, Bijou? Are you hungry at this hour? Can't it wait?" Angela said, standing pat as her little dachshund friend pulled harder against the leash. "Do you need a drink of water? Let's make it quick."

They headed into the dark kitchen. Angela turned on the light, put the laptop on the shiny stainless workspace, and dropped the leash as she filled a flat dish with water. Bijou ran to the door of the walk-in refrigerator and began to scratch on the bottom panel.

"Bijou, what could you want in there?"

Angela glanced next at the freshly opened bag of Bijou's favorite fancy kibble. It was not far from the door of the walk-in, but Bijou was completely ignoring it.

Angela put the dish on the floor and walked to the refrigerator. She reached for the handle and gasped.

Is that blood?

She yanked the door open and cried out as Bijou ran in. Aseem was on the floor: silent, motionless, and bleeding from his head.

She crouched down and gently shook his shoulder. "Wake up, darling, wake up!" she said, but Aseem didn't respond. Bijou sweetly sniffed at Aseem's face and softly nudged his neck with her tiny snout.

Shaking with fear, Angela's mind went blank for a moment. But then she pulled her phone from her pocket and called 911.

"Yes—I think he's breathing," she said into the phone. "But he's not responding. Please hurry!"

LEXIE HAD PARKED HER CAR ON THE SIDE OF THE road about a hundred yards from Heavenly West, hoping she wasn't visible from the property, even as she kept her own eyes trained on it. After sitting more than half an hour in the pitch dark,

Lexie was getting tired and frustrated—and wondering if she'd miscalculated.

Tailing DJ Tad's van to Napa had been the easy part, though she'd been surprised when he cruised right past the inn and up the hill to Connie Hollander's place. As they'd turned off the freeway onto the wine country road toward the inn, she'd grinned as she realized her guess had been right. The money and whatever else he'd exchanged with the limo driver had something to do with the murder at the inn.

As the van turned into the small parking lot of Heavenly West, Lexie had kept her eyes forward and driven past the driveway purposefully, not wanting to be spotted by Tad. She'd turned her headlights off as soon as she hit a bend, hoping no other vehicles would appear on the lonely road, and spun a quick U-turn and found a spot on the shoulder. She managed to be quiet about it—she was practically holding her breath in the car. Thanks to the overhead light in his van, she'd spied Tad hopping out of his van, and he seemed no wiser to her presence just up the road. She'd clenched her fists and grinned with pleasure.

Yes!

Then Tad made it all so much easier for her. At first, she could barely make out his shape as he walked toward the partly built home off the edge of the parking area. But Tad managed to trip a motion-sensitive light, positioning himself perfectly underneath it.

Haha! Quite the criminal mastermind, Tad!

Lexie strained her eyes for a sign of Tad once that light went out. She saw him slip into the shell of the garage—and then, nothing.

He's tampering with something. Do I dare creep over for a look? What if he spots me? Or what if he leaves and I lose him?

She'd decided not to chance any of that—so now here she was, half an hour later, bored, frustrated, and anxious.

Technically, it's thirty-six minutes later. And counting.

She didn't dare make a call or send a text, for fear that Tad was still there and would spot the light. Her car was becoming oppressively stuffy, but she didn't even dare open the window to let in some of the crisp, clean night air. The wine country night was so serene, even the sound of her power window might be audible yards away.

What was that sound? A crunch on the bits of gravel on the Heavenly West parking lot?

She heard, then saw, the DJ hustling clumsily toward his van, then sliding the side door open with a clunk and a whoosh. In the shadowy light of the vehicle's overhead lamp, she saw Tad toss something large in the back, then something smaller that landed with a clank. Then he hustled into the cab and started the engine. Lexie waited until he'd roared out of the lot before starting her car, though Tad seemed so focused on rushing away, she wondered if he would even have noticed if she drove right after him.

As she followed at a careful distance behind Tad, his van careening too fast around the bend past the inn, Lexie pondered her next move—or rather, her next call.

Do I call Bea or Sergeant McGregor?

As her car sailed over a hump in the road, she decided the answer was obvious.

Jeez, dude! Better get you arrested before you kill us both!

ASEEM REGAINED CONSCIOUSNESS IN THE ambulance, and by the time they got to the hospital, he was insisting he'd be fine back home at the inn.

"Very brave," said the EMT. "But at a minimum, you need stitches for that cut. And I know the docs will want to check you out for concussion—at least. You were knocked out, after all."

"See, it's settled," Angela said quietly, holding his hand. "And you didn't even have to hear it from me."

"You should probably try to rest," the EMT said. "We'll be at the hospital in no time."

Once Aseem's head wound was sutured and covered with gauze, an orderly wheeled him to a cramped private room. "You got a nasty conk on the cranium," the avuncular emergency doctor said. "We'd better keep an eye on you overnight. Try to rest."

"You heard what the doctor said," Angela said. She was standing at the side of the bed. "You look tired. You should sleep. But first, I want to say how sorry I am. Our fight—it was all my fault. I should have trusted you." She teared up as she said it. Aseem reached for her hand, and lightly intertwined his fingers in hers.

"No, I'm sorry. It was my fault. I should've told you where I was going. I didn't expect it to amount to anything. Who thinks that when Gary Wheaton invites you to pitch your ideas, your first meeting will actually be with... *Gary Wheaton?*" Aseem laughed as he said it, then winced and touched his hand to his head.

"Painkillers not kicking in yet?" Angela said. "I'll call the nurse—"

"It's fine, just don't make me laugh. I'm getting tired, Angel, but I want to finish explaining.

"I didn't want to look foolish. Foolish to you, I mean. That's all it was. You've done so much with the inn and the publishing business, I'm so proud of you every day. I guess I just… I didn't want to be that joker whose girlfriend is out of his league. I mean, it sounds dumb now that I hear myself say it out loud."

"You could never be that!"

"I want you to know I'm honored to work with you on your business, Angel. I wasn't looking for a job. I have ideas of my own, but I thought a wild dream might be to get a little investment from Gary in one of my apps. As in, enough to do a little marketing, or maybe hire a buddy to help me code it, to keep it going on the side. Gary offering me a full-time job—talk about out of left field—"

"Not really," Angela said, holding his hand more tightly. "Gary only saw the brilliance the rest of us see."

"I was flattered, of course. Who wouldn't be? But, Angel, I told him I can't—I won't—let you down. I told him I couldn't accept a full-time job with him and leave Betty Snickerdoodle, Inc. behind."

"Aseem… I… I'm not sure you should have done that," Angela said, her eyes wide and brow furrowed. "I realized something, too. Don't you want the chance to build something of your own? It's what we both always talked about—don't you remember, when we first met?"

"Of course I do."

"And now you've turned down a huge opportunity to do it… from *Gary Wheaton*?! All for me? I don't think you should have!" Angela looked distraught. "I shouldn't have pressured you. What was I thinking?" She pulled her fingers from his and put her face in her hands.

"Angel, trust me, you're wrong."

"I wish there was something you could do to take it back. Don't you want to work for Gary? He's one of your idols!"

"Are you serious? You really wish I had decided to work for Gary?"

"Yes—I mean, assuming you want to. I'm so lucky to have you helping me, sweetheart—but it can't come at the expense of your dreams."

"Well, good. Because that's where you're wrong. I didn't tell Gary I couldn't work for him —I just said I'd work part-time for you at the inn, and part-time on his incubator. And he was fine with it."

"Aseem... what you're telling me is, you said no, I want different terms, to the CEO of a Fortune 100 company? Who's also your idol?"

"I like to think of it as negotiating," Aseem said, grinning.

"You're amazing. And it's... it's perfect. And I want you to promise me something," Angela said. "If—I mean, when—your apps, or the incubator, or anything you're working on with Gary takes off, you must promise me—I mean, *must*—that you will run with it. Even if it means I have to stand on my own two feet alone."

"You'll never be alone if I can help it, Angel. Regardless of whether we pursue our own things."

Angela leaned over and kissed him on the cheek. "We'll never be alone. And we'll figure this out together, won't we? Because I've never been in love before, either."

Aseem smiled and kissed her lightly, but then pulled back. "Wait—have you been reading my email?" His face looked serious.

"I'm sorry—I was looking for you, and the email was open on the laptop—and it was addressed to me—"

Aseem smiled. "Just teasing you, Angel. Let's

face it, if you hadn't read it, I'd be going hypothermic in that fridge. And I trust you with my life—"

"Boundaries—something we have to figure out together."

"Lots to learn, my love. I'm looking forward to all of it."

CHAPTER 17

"Angel. Wake up."

Despite contorting herself like a pretzel to curl up in the hospital room's small, rigid guest chair, Angela had managed to fall into a deep sleep for an hour or two, after the last time a nurse came in to check on Aseem.

Angela stretched and opened her bleary eyes to find Aseem awake and Bea and Connie standing at the foot of his bed.

"Morning, Sunshine," Connie said, handing her friend a paper cup of fragrant coffee. Aseem watched intently as the cup moved from Connie's hand to Angela's. "Sorry, Aseem, I would have brought one for you, but I wasn't sure if you were allowed to have one."

"Don't worry about him. I'm sure room service in this joint is fabulous," Bea said.

"No worries," Aseem said, pushing the button to lift up the head of his bed. "I need to get up and out of here, anyway. I've got to tell the police who hit me."

"No need for that. McGregor knows. DJ Tad, right?"

"Yes. I saw him sneaking down the trail from Heavenly West and followed him to the kitchen. But how do *you* know?" Aseem said.

"Did he hit you with that big mixer bowl?" Bea said.

"I don't think so — it was something with a sharp edge. That's how my head got cut."

"Plus, that bowl is super heavy—hard to picture someone swinging it, even a guy who works out as much as Tad," Angela added.

"Well then, it must have been the pan with the chicken wings," Bea proclaimed.

"What? The chicken wing container?" Angela said, her face scrunched. "Hmm. I think I saw a chicken wing on the floor of the walk-in. Bijou was so concerned about Aseem that she ignored it."

"That's my girl," Connie said. "Bijou loves her food, but not as much as she loves a good man.

She would have left my ex for dead for a lot less than a chicken wing."

"How do you know all of this, Bea?" Aseem said.

Bea sighed dramatically and looked up at the ceiling. "It's not ideal. This room is all wrong. And no offense, but you three aren't much of an audience. But I suppose the time has come for my big reveal." Bea spoke in the manner of someone bravely soldiering on, triggering an irrepressible snicker from Connie.

"Sorry, Bea," she giggled. "Please continue."

"Drat! I forgot my cane! It's really going to be a challenge to maintain my customary presentation standards. I can only ask that you bear with me as I try."

Bea patted the pocket of her eggplant-colored velour track suit and smiled. "With no cane, I suppose this prop will have to do." Then she pulled out a large, filigree button and presented it to each member of her modest audience in the ostentatious manner of a carnival magician.

"It was this little clue—this seemingly meaningless, everyday object—that started me on the hunt for our poisoner," Bea began. "The trail was tricky, naturally. This button pointed solidly in the direction of deservedly dead Rhonda. Of course, we didn't know she was dead at the time—what we knew was that she was a fearsome bully who threatened people to get her way. Poisoning her own colleagues to secure a better deal on weddings at the inn seemed right up her alley. So this was my initial theory."

"Bea, you've had that this whole time? Shouldn't you have given it to Sergeant McGregor? It must have been evidence," Angela asked.

"Fair point, girlie. But you're forgetting that at that time, the only crime we knew about was the poisoning at our inn. And even that mischief was only just dawning on us, thanks to that silly inspector for hire, and the unexpected help of Lexie."

"And McGregor laughed at the idea of investigating it," Angela said, nodding.

"Egg-zactly!" Bea said, thrusting her hand, and the button, toward the ceiling. "We were on our own. So off we went to Sacramento, where I was determined to find more proof that Rhonda was our poisoner. You, of course, were driven primarily by wedding fever—"

"Bea!" Angela cried. "I told you, I do not have wedding fever!" She looked fearfully at Aseem, but relaxed once she saw he was laughing.

"Oh dear," Bea said, leaning in to scrutinize

Aseem's face at a completely inappropriate distance. "You seem so at ease with the idea. Has the nurse taken your temperature this morning? In your weakened condition, could Angie have passed the fever on to you?"

"We do not have wedding fever, Bea." Angela looked at Bea with as stern a face as she could muster.

"Perhaps it's best to proceed with my analysis," Bea said. She backed away from the head of Aseem's bed and resumed pacing the floor.

"I'm still waiting to hear how you knew it was DJ Tad," Aseem said. "And how McGregor knows, too."

"All shall be revealed," Bea said, waving her magic button around again. "Fast-forward to our visit to Sacramento. Rhonda no-shows for the wedding, and Angie's old friend Georgie is wearing white gloves. Neither of us properly interpreted these clues, however. I was too convinced Rhonda was hiding out, while we now know she was actually dead, and Angie, as she's inclined to do, had faith in her old friend."

Angela frowned until Connie piped up, "It's one of your better traits, honey."

"This button was not the only clue, though. Angela's sharp eyes had spotted the little bag of leftover leaves—a crucial discovery! They turned out to be needleweed, our poison, since confirmed by our new friend Fiona."

Angela looked pleased with herself, her smile restored.

"Fiona told us about the thorns. Still assuming our villainess Rhonda was behind the crime, I smugly believed the blood on the whipped cream bowl must have been hers. Here was proof, I thought, that Rhonda had pricked herself with her poison plants while sabotaging the salads. But I was wrong—"

"Because we next caught Georgina red-handed, literally, with the garden shears in Rhonda's yard, where all that needleweed was growing," Angela interjected. She turned to Aseem to add, "And now she's even admitted to the poisoning."

"Partly right, Angie," Bea said, nodding pompously. "Partly right."

"Is this where DJ Tad comes in?" Aseem said.

"Interesting point, handsome. DJ Tad was with Georgina in Rhonda's garden. But we're still skipping an important part of the story—and that's your part, Connie."

"Me? You mean discovering Rhonda's body?"

"That's a very important part, of course. But before that, you discovered a strange car in your new garage. Whose was it, and how did it get there? Another piece, as it turned out, that would need to fit in the puzzle."

"Next we find Rhonda—or rather, Bijou and Connie find Rhonda—in the barn," Angela said.

"Yes. And two and two seemed to go together—Angie, you thought because we now knew that Georgina was the poisoner, she must have done the murder as well."

"McGregor thought so, too. She had the motive." Angela said.

"And I agreed, at first. But that's when I made my most brilliant deduction yet!" Bea waved the button above her head triumphantly. "The key to the entire case!"

Angela sighed indulgently. "Don't keep us waiting. The suspense is killing us."

"Angie, recall that there was no evidence that Rhonda had been dragged from the pile of chicken bones—the ones by the chicken coop, which we assumed were the remains of her snack. But if her body wasn't dragged from there, how'd she get under that vat?"

"She might have been lured into the barn by her killer—"

"She might have, except for one crucial fact of timing. The rental company didn't come to pick up the furniture in the barn until after the mixer ended—long after Rhonda went missing. But if Rhonda had been stuffed under the wine barrel before the end of the mixer, the rental people would have noticed her. At the very least, they would have noticed her ugly foot," Bea said, guffawing and slapping her knee. "That told me that she was probably killed elsewhere and stashed somewhere safe until after the mixer—"

"The walk-in," blurted Aseem.

"Exactly, Aseem. You're even smarter than you look. And I should add that you provided another crucial clue."

"I did?"

"Your conversation with Paige. That told us it wasn't just the caterers and Georgina and Rhonda who had access to the kitchen, it was also the handful of people who wouldn't have a chance to eat during the event, such as—"

"The DJs!" Aseem and Angela said at once.

"So I figured one of the DJs finds Rhonda in the kitchen, in the middle of whipping the cream for Paige—"

"Wait, how do we know that?" Angela said.

"Paige told me," Aseem said. "She said she'd set the cream up so that it could be whipped just before dessert was served, and since she was swamped with serving, Rhonda offered to turn the cream on to whip for a few minutes, then turn it off."

"Another brilliant observation from your boyfriend, Angie. If only you'd been speaking to him at the time, you'd have heard it directly from him."

Angela shrugged and mouthed "sorry" at Aseem.

"That ancient behemoth of a mixer is the perfect thing for breaking a lady's neck," Bea said. "It doesn't have the safety guard a newer machine would have. I think that's how Rhonda lost her pretty button—and her *life*." Bea melodramatically dragged the last word out to two or three syllables.

"You think Tad pushed her head in the mixer?"

"Yep. I think he saw his opportunity and shoved her when her back was turned. Maybe he didn't even intend to kill her, just scare her—like a taste of her own medicine. But then her clothing got caught, and crackle-crunch-crunch went the neck bones."

"Ew, Bea," Angela winced.

"The move was impulsive, though, so now he had to scramble. After shoving Rhonda's dead body into the fridge—I think he wheeled her in, still upside down in the bowl, the bowl on its dolly —Tad needed to deal with some pesky details. He took Rhonda's phone from her pocket and used it to text Georgina saying, 'I'm leaving.' And he texted Paige to say ixnay on the essertday.

"That part was easy. But what if someone saw her van parked at Heavenly West? Tad had to hide it somewhere, but couldn't leave the mixer, because he was one of the DJs running the show. He needed an accomplice—someone who could quickly go to your place, Connie, and move the van. It had to be someone who wouldn't be missed. Smart money says it was the limo driver. No one would notice he'd gone, because he was staying mostly outside during the mixer, anyway —in case anyone needed a shuttle to Heavenly West."

"What about Rhonda's body? How did Tad get it to the barn?" Aseem asked.

"I think I know," Angela said. "Those wheeled cases the DJs used to move their stuff in and out— remember how you heard somebody wheeling stuff out long after the mixer was over?"

"My thoughts exactly, Angie. I thought I heard Tad and Cam wheeling loads outside my window late at night. Maybe Tad stalled and deliberately finished late. That way, he could make an extra trip with one of his trunks over to the barn, and the noise would be camouflaged among the rest of his loads."

"With Rhonda stuffed inside?" gasped Connie. "Oh, my stars!"

"What about the chicken wings? Are you saying he stopped to snack on wings after rolling Rhonda to the barn?"

"Good question, Angie. Might have been convenient, since they were both in the fridge. Rhonda and the wings, I mean," Bea snorted. "But I think Tad might have gone out for a little walk with his snack earlier and spied on the rental company as they moved the tables out. He was probably anxious to find a place to shove Rhonda's corpse where it wouldn't be found for a few days."

"Maybe McGregor will be able to get DNA off those wings."

"I hope Dames and Paprika didn't chew it all off," Connie said.

"Shall we head back to the inn and find out? McGregor & Co are there right now, confirming my theory as we speak."

Angela snorted. "Does McGregor work for you now?"

"It's fine with me if he thinks we're partners."

They arrived back at the inn and Connie parked next to the police van. After the four of them—Bea, Connie, Angela, and Aseem—piled out of her car, Connie went to her suite to check on Bijou and the pups, and Aseem headed to his own for a shower. Bea and Angela headed straight for the barn to see what McGregor and his junior officer had learned.

"Isn't that Lexie's car?" Angela said, pointing to the car on the other side of the cruiser. "What's she doing here?"

"She's covering the murder for the *Grapevine,* right? Plus, she's been helping me out with a little project," Bea said.

"You're doing a side project with Lexie?" Angela said, her cheeks flushing.

"Now girlie, don't worry. Think of it like Lexie's doing the dirty work and… and we get the benefit. I'll tell you all about it later."

As they reached the barn they found Lexie standing at the edge of the trail, observing McGregor and his team at work on the scene. Officer Carroll was standing by the chicken coop, carefully photographing the area where the wing bones were found.

"Found another bone," Carroll yelled to McGregor.

"Bag it up!" McGregor called from the barn.

"Do they think they'll get Tad's DNA from that chicken wing?" Angela asked Lexie.

"They've got a few possibilities. I tipped McGregor off to Tad leaving Heavenly West last night, and when they nabbed him on the freeway, they found a few choice items from your kitchen in his van, including the mixing bowl and the pan Tad clocked Aseem with. Is Aseem doing OK, by the way?"

"He's going to be fine. I took pictures of the mixing bowl before I washed it. Maybe I don't have to feel so bad about destroying evidence now that Tad has revealed how much he wanted to get rid of the bowl. And that chicken wing pan probably has Aseem's blood on it, too. More evidence."

"Exactly. Maybe Tad's prints, also. Luckily, I called McGregor in time for him to intercept Tad and prevent him from destroying that evidence."

"Listen, Lexie, I know you and Beatrice want to take credit for solving this one, but I'd already received an alert that the victim's phone was pinging again," McGregor shouted inside the barn. "As soon as Tad dropped the phone back in Rhonda's van and turned it on, the wheels were in motion."

Lexie leaned toward Bea and Angela and whispered, "He's saying that now. But when the dispatcher put me through to him last night, he was not on Tad's trail. He sounded like he'd been asleep."

"You got to wake Lazybones up and put him to work? Some girls have all the luck!" Bea cackled.

"I heard that, Sickles!"

The three of them moved near the barn door and watched McGregor lean down with a grunt to take closer pictures of the area where Rhonda had been found. A county technician, dressed head to toe in protective garb, was swabbing the wine cask for DNA samples. One spot on the barrel had already been dusted for a visible fingerprint.

"Why would Tad turn Rhonda's phone back on? Sounds like he was hoping to get caught," Angela whispered to Lexie.

"I think he was trying to frame his accomplice," Lexie whispered back. Then she leaned over the yellow tape blocking the door and said to McGregor, "Find the candy-related evidence yet, Sarge? You're still going to need me to tell you how it ended up where you found it—and why."

"That's called being a witness, missy," McGregor said. "Surely you're not planning to obstruct the investigation of a murder, are you? I know you journalists like to think of yourselves as rebels, but even an ambitious youngster like you must have limits."

Lexie winked at Bea and Angela and shrugged. "We'll see, Sarge. In the meantime, I suggest you handle any chocolate wrappers with care. They're evidence of someone being framed."

"Why can't you just admit you couldn't solve this thing without us ladies, McGreggy?" Bea said. "Angela had a piece of the puzzle, too. Without her, you'd probably still be assuming Georgina did it."

"If you aren't going to be helpful, Sickles, why don't you and your gal pals leave us alone to do our job?"

The three of them walked toward the inn. "Lexie, why'd you tell him about the chocolate bars? You could have saved that for our project," Bea said, once they were out of the cops' earshot.

"Couldn't really let the limo driver get framed for murder, could I? Don't worry, we've still got lots of juice. Like the real reason Tad did it—and the connection to that other wedding industry scam I've been investigating. Plenty of good stuff for our book." Lexie leaned her shoulder toward Bea, wearing a self-satisfied smile.

"Your book?" Angela said, scanning both of their faces.

"Oh Angie, don't be jelly," Bea said, grinning like a child trying out a new toy.

"Jelly? *Jelly?*" Angela cried.

Bea winked at Lexie. "It's how the kids say 'jealous,' Angie."

"I know that!" Angela rolled her eyes and sighed loudly.

"Angie, it's *our* book, as in the three of us," Bea said. "I'm the editor and I get credit for the concept. Lexie's the author, and she's going to write a nice series based on it for the *Grapevine*. How are the two of us going to get it to market without our secret weapon—you, our publisher?"

Angela's expression softened. "You could have clued me in earlier."

"We didn't know if there was enough story for a book," Lexie said. "At first, Bea just asked me to look into the wedding fair scam she heard about from Sandy Givens. The one that got Rhonda all riled up when Dennis mentioned it. I thought it might make a good investigative article—"

"And I thought it might make a good story for my next mystery book," Bea said.

"We didn't know there'd be so much to the story—or that it would wind up being connected to Rhonda's murder."

"We're going to need a new imprint for nonfiction," Angela said.

"Betty Snickerdoodle True Crime is too long," Bea said. "How about BS True Crime?"

Lexie and Angela burst out laughing. "'BS' may not be the best brand for nonfiction. Besides," Angela added, "If this true crime idea takes off, maybe we'll bring on authors to write about serial killers or who knows what. I don't think we want sweet Betty's brand associated with all that."

"See? You're thinking big again, Angie. I love it!" Bea squealed, giving her knee a slap.

Angela furrowed her brow and cocked her head. "I've got it: Big Reveal Publishing."

"Love it," Lexie said.

"Speaking of big reveals, Lexie, what were you saying about the wedding fair scam being connected to Rhonda's murder? I thought that con happened in Chicago."

"It was in Chicago—and before that, in Providence, and before that, in Seattle and a couple other cities. The scammers stayed a step ahead of the law and the press. The amounts each vendor lost were mostly in the hundreds of dollars, or low four figures in some cases. The losses were enough to damage small wedding businesses, even cripple some of them, but not enough to give the investigations staying power. But when you add it all up, they stole hundreds of thousands of dollars.

"You've probably figured out by now that Rhonda was the mastermind of the con. She came to Sacramento thinking bigger, it looks like—figuring she'd make one more quick hit and move on fast to a new town, with a new identity—"

"But Dennis spooked her, poor guy," Bea said. "He was unlucky enough to be right."

"Yep. And then there was the fake fair's beleaguered sales rep, who decided enough was enough. A person no one ever met, and everyone knew only by a male email handle, but one familiar to any good college girl who studied her women's fiction. George—"

Angela gasped. "George Sand?"

"'Fraid so," Lexie said. "The light bulb went off for me when I saw that, first 'cuz of the women's fiction connection, plus it just seemed odd that a guy would be selling space at a bridal fair. And I immediately started thinking pseudonyms, like, 'George, Georgina. George, Georgina.'"

"Oh, Georgina. So much for straightening up and flying right," Angela sighed.

"She was trying, girlie. She wanted to stop the scam and strike out on her own. Rhonda wasn't having any of it, though."

"My guess is Rhonda threatened to reveal the scam and pin the entire thing on Georgina unless she stayed under her thumb."

"But I don't get it. We know Tad killed Rhonda, don't we? What's the motive?"

"The oldest story in the book," Bea said. "True love. At least on Tad's part. Georgina wasn't on board for anything more than friendship, but she'd gotten used to him taking care of her."

"You're not saying—" Angela said, aghast.

"No, no—she had no idea he'd go that far," Lexie said. "I'm sure of it."

"Pretty good story, though—right, Angie?" Bea said.

"I guess that depends on your point of view. But from the publisher perspective, it sure is."

: CHAPTER 18

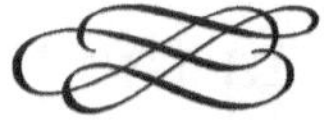

In three months' time, thanks to the combination of Lexie's dogged reporting, Bea's brilliance in spotting the story, and Angela's marketing magic, Betty Snickerdoodle's new true-crime publishing imprint found itself at the center of the book event of the year.

Angela had created so much hype about the new imprint and its first book, anyone who was anyone clamored for a ticket to the late-summer launch event at Betty Snickerdoodle's Christmas Inn & Ranch. And now the big day was here, and the ballroom was packed with Northern California media movers and shakers: book reviewers, local news organizations, bookstore owners.

Looking official in her faithful security guard ensemble, Pat stood at the end of a velvet rope checking tickets, to make sure no uninvited guests joined the party—and to reinforce the air of exclusivity.

Inside the ballroom, guests enjoyed fancy cocktails and top-shelf networking while they waited for Lexie and Bea's joint reading. Two podiums were set up on the stage, one on each side of the massive video display. In the back of the room, in front of the giant fireplace and between two elegantly decorated Christmas trees, Angela had set up two long tables, both piled with hardcovers, for Lexie and Bea to do book signings. Huge stacks of books stood behind the tables. Angela was standing near the tables, fiddling with them, making sure everything was just right.

"Wow, Angie, think we've got enough books?" Bea said. "I hope Lexie's been doing her finger stretches. She's got a lot of autographing to do."

"This is just the beginning," Angela said. "We've had nearly as many preorders as for one of your Treacle Town books. And once the big news comes out, I predict sales will go even higher."

"No doubt. Just wait 'til Lexie hears we've been short-listed for a California journalism prize. I pity her bosses at the *Grapevine*. That girl's gonna negotiate."

"Probably too late. Did you see the editor from the *Sacramento Bee* is here? He said he's already made Lexie an offer. And Lexie told me herself that she's got an interview next week at the *Los Angeles Times*. But speaking of negotiating, how'd you persuade Lexie to do the twin outfits?" Angela asked Bea. "Especially, you know, *that* outfit?"

Lexie and Bea were both wearing customized track suits made of plush, silvery velour. On the back of the jacket "Big Reveal Publishing Presents…" was printed in rhinestones—a replica of the image on the gigantic video display on the ballroom stage.

"Nice you let her customize a little, though," Angela chuckled. "She's managed to sex it up." Lexie's version of the outfit had the jacket unzipped from the bottom and arranged so that her midriff was exposed from her bustline to her waistband. And unlike Bea's velcro sneakers, Lexie's kitten-heel booties were designed for style, not comfort.

"You did a nice thing, too, Angie, inviting some of the wedding professionals to join in."

Paige had set up a long table full of delicious appetizers, which were also being passed by servers walking around the room. Sandy Givens was taking photos. Ethel Bennett—the elderly harpist with the heart condition—was a guest of honor, happily fully recovered from her poisoning ordeal. And Dennis Poundstone's former DJ, now on his own, was standing near the stage, playing upbeat music and preparing for the presentation.

"Don't think we'll be having weddings here anytime soon, but it's nice to give them some positive press. I think that Paige's business is still hurting from all the online chatter about the poisoning. I still feel terrible about what happened to Dennis."

"Sandy said she heard from him, and that he and his wife love Alaska," Bea said. "He sent her a picture of the two of them from the state fair, standing in front of a one-ton pumpkin. I think he's enjoying the next adventure."

"It's just so unfair. He'd been nothing but an upstanding guy in their industry, yet people were all too happy to pile on when Rhonda decided to tear him down."

"Sometimes perception becomes reality, Angie."

"Yes, exactly. Dennis gets driven out of business, and Georgina gets probation."

"She hit the jackpot with that middle-aged

male judge. Natural beauty has its privileges. She has to stay out of the wedding industry for five years, though. That'll make things harder for her."

"She claimed she was looking for a fresh start," Angela scoffed. "At least she took responsibility and apologized. Let's hope that if anyone trusts her again, she won't repay them by conning them. I can't believe I ever trusted her. At least I wasn't the only sucker this time."

"The way I see it, you're lucky in this life if you can trust yourself and maybe a few other people. It's good to have goals, but don't imagine too much is under your control. Most you can do is try your best—like you *always* do, Angie. And—might I humbly suggest—have fun while doing it. We only get our one ride on the blue marble—"

"The blue marble again? More poker wisdom?" Angela rolled her eyes but smiled. "I know, I know, I have lots to enjoy and plenty of reasons to be grateful."

"Speaking of which, there's several of them." Bea tipped her head toward a group that had gathered by the ballroom's enormous French doors: their personal VIP guests. Angela and Bea walked over to join them.

Aseem and Connie were there, of course, plus Angela's mother, Maria; Charlie Carter, Bea's dear friend and first literary agent; and Perry James, who ran the Valley Card Room and was Bea's old pal (and maybe more?) from her days as a poker professional long ago.

Perry had come straight from work and was still dressed in a suit and tie. He carried a canvas sack that looked almost like an old-fashioned money bag. It was stuffed and bulging.

"I brought Pat's pay," he said, showing it to Bea. He shook the bag, producing the unmistakable sound of poker chips clattering against each other. "All one-dollar chips, just like you asked."

"Good, makes it seem like more!" Bea said.

"Bea, does Pat ever complain when you pay her in poker chips?" Connie said.

"Why would she? Works out great for both of us. I pay her twice her regular rate when I pay her in chips. 'Course, then we go down to the cardroom and I win it all back."

"She doesn't mind?"

"Nah. She's learning to play poker from the best. Like I always say, there's no such thing as free lessons in poker—or in life," Bea said, with another laugh. "Besides, she sometimes picks up a few bucks from the other players and comes out ahead."

Not far from the book tables, Fiona and Gary

Wheaton were standing together, clearly enjoying themselves. Gary moved behind Fee and put his arms around her in a way that suggested true devotion—with an undercurrent of enduring passion. Unconsciously, Aseem did the same to Angela, and they swayed along to the DJ's music.

"So, Bea," Angela said. "We've got news. We've set a date."

"I knew it! You passed your affliction on to Aseem! When is it—"

Maria gulped and stared at her daughter, eyes wide. Angela smiled and winked at her.

"Don't be silly, Bea. We didn't set a date to get *married*. We set a date for me to meet Aseem's parents."

"Getting married could be in our future," Aseem said. "But first things first. We don't need to rush."

"Meeting your parents is a big enough deal for now." Angela smiled. "Plus, bluffing you, Bea, is always good fun. You do admit that I just bluffed you, don't you?"

"As long as you're having a good time, girlie, I'm all for it," Bea said.

Charlie grabbed one of the books off the table. "Unusual title, Bea. I like it. How'd you come up with it?"

"Just seemed to fit. I wanted to call it *You Schmooze, You Lose*, but Angela thought that would seem a little tasteless—you know, given the *financial ruin* and the *poisoning* and the *murder*," Bea said, unleashing an extra noisy cackle that carried over the hum of the crowd. "You know I'm all about tastefulness, Charlie."

The DJ briefly dimmed the lights and asked everyone who wanted to sit for the readings to move to the rows of chairs in front of the stage.

"Almost show time, Angie," Bea said. "Be sure to listen to the music the DJ plays for our walk-on. It's dedicated to you from me."

The DJ began playing "Hold On Loosely" and dimmed the lights down again. Bea said, "That's our cue." She and Lexie started walking toward the stairs at each end of the stage.

Bea turned back for a moment and shouted back toward Angela, "Listen to the song. 'Hold On Loosely' means don't be jelly, Angie!"

Angela laughed and rolled her eyes. "Oh, brother! I know what it means." Aseem kissed her on the cheek, seemingly unaware of Bea's unsubtle reminder.

Then as Bea and Lexie reached the podiums, the audience applauded enthusiastically. The DJ introduced them and switched up the graphic to show off the cover of their highly anticipated book:

WEDDING FEVER:
How greed, envy, and unrequited love brought fraud and murder to America's sweetest industry

"Ask anyone who works in the wedding industry, in any part of the country, and you'll hear that it's filled with gentle, romantic souls who are in it to celebrate love—not get rich," Lexie began. "Like any community of mostly good-hearted, trusting people, though, the wedding industry isn't impervious to con artists—nor to jealous people blinded by desire. In this sad and unlikely story of avarice and lust, we find that some people in this gentle world could even be driven to *murder* for what they desperately wanted.

"But let's start at the beginning, with the stories of our three main characters: A conniving, opportunistic wedding planner, consumed with desire for money and power. Her beautiful, entitled, immature apprentice. And the man, blinded by passion, who thought if he could eliminate one, he might be able to captivate the other...."

- The End -

FROM THE AUTHOR

Thank you for choosing and reading my book!

If you enjoyed it, I hope you'll consider leaving a rating or review on Amazon, Goodreads or Book-Bub. Reader reviews help others discover new books they'll enjoy.

I love staying in touch with readers! If you'd like to connect, please sign up for my newsletter at pepperfrostauthor.com

or just email me: pepper@pepperfrostauthor.com.

By signing up for my newsletter, you'll be alerted when my next release is ready. Another way to be among the first to know is to follow me on Bookbub at bookbub.com/authors/pepper-frost.

I'm so grateful for your support! If you have feedback you'd like to share with me, I hope you'll get in touch.

♥ Pepper